THE SELKIE SCANDAL

A PREQUEL NOVELLA TO THE LADY DIVINER SERIES

ROSALIE OAKS

Parkerville
PRESS

CONTENTS

CHAPTER 1

Jaq

The High Prince of Skerry had a sore head, and he was fairly certain it was from the excessive consumption of coral cutthroat.

In fact, Jaq's whole body hurt, which was somewhat unusual. Without opening his eyes, he wriggled his extremities. Very carefully. A faint sense of fingers met his consciousness. Oh good. And his other appendages, including feet, were all present and correct.

He had reverted to human form, then, for the moment. Perhaps seal form would be better. Jaq groaned. Transforming would be painful, but maybe it was worth it if the seal fat would absorb some alcohol. He must have partaken liberally yesterday.

Yet, from what he recalled, he had not drunk enough to feel like *this*.

Jaq lay there a moment longer, realising he was naked (his usual state after transforming to human). He could feel rough fabric: a blanket over his limbs. Not that he really needed it to keep warm; being a selkie was useful in that way. Vaguely, he wondered who had placed it there.

"Awake, are you?" A voice disturbed Jaq's cogitations, and he opened his eyes.

The merman who had spoken to him was very attractive. This was no surprise, as all mermen were very attractive: long, muscled, lithe, and fine-boned. It was why Jaq liked spending time with them: they were almost as beautiful as him. This merman had blue-green skin and pale green hair lying lank on his back. Jaq recognised him: Fenner, who was a bit too fast at dolphin races for Jaq's liking.

Fenner propped his elbows on the same rock that Jaq occupied, leaning slightly out of the water, his long tail gently swirling in the water. His gaze was contemptuous. "Conscious?"

"Mrgh. Barely."

"You overdid it yesterday."

"It was my sister's birthday." This, surely, was some excuse.

Fenner grinned. "Embarrassed yourself?"

"Did I?" Jaq rather suspected he had. To stop that train of thought, he pushed his black hair out of his face and examined his surroundings. They were unfamiliar: a cave with long slabs of stone sloping into the water and a shallow roof sweeping overhead. The glow-worms hurt his eyes, so he shut them again. "Where am I?"

"We thought we'd take you somewhere you don't know," said Fenner.

Jaq squinted and wondered why.

Fenner continued. "The others are in the outer cave. Do you want to join us?"

"For a game?"

"Yes, we've got cards and bones. And more drink, if you like."

Jaq grimaced. "Scale of the fish? No, I thank you. I'll rest a bit." Not to mention he was already deep in debt to this particular pod of mermen.

"Sorry for the secrecy … and the rope." Fenner's voice was faintly apologetic. "Costo said we should do the thing properly."

Jaq lifted his head in sudden inquiry and twitched the blanket off his legs. Amid a surging throb in his temple, he saw his feet were loosely bound in a long merrope. It trailed over the edge of the rock into the water.

"What the devil … ?" Jaq scrambled to sitting, and

the rope tightened. "Why in hell's desert have you tied me up?"

"You have been taken hostage, Your Highness, if I may remind you," said Fenner with a smirk. "You are worth a pretty penny right now, and we intend to make the most of it."

Jaq slunk back onto his rock, recalling certain events and eyeing both Fenner and the rope with disfavour. "You didn't need to tie me up."

"We wanted to be sure you wouldn't abandon us."

Jaq twitched a brow. "You've got cards, haven't you? And didn't you mention a drink?"

CHAPTER 2

Beresford

The Earl of Beresford was having cream tea with his mother. He took a long gulp and tried not to let his eyes drift to the small curve of the ocean, far beyond the manicured gardens.

They were partaking of the famous estate plum jam, but unlike the rest of England, Beresford had eaten enough of the stuff to last his whole lifetime. He sighed and settled his broad shoulders against the settee.

"Pass the jam, dear boy," said the countess. She proceeded to spoon out a generous dollop of the plum jam onto her chudleigh (a yeast leavened bun), which was already lavishly topped with clotted cream. "And tell me, why are you in Devon instead of London?"

"To keep you company, of course," Beresford countered. "Why shouldn't I be in my ancestral seat?"

"You ought to be looking for a bride." The Countess of Beresford took a bite of cream, jam, and chudleigh, but her sharp grey eyes stayed fixed on her son. They shared the same eye colour: sea grey. It went nicely with his mother's silver-white hair but probably just looked odd with his chestnut brown.

Beresford took a sip of tea, delaying his answer. "Brides are boring."

"Nonsense. You simply have not found the right woman. What is more, you have not looked. You lark about the countryside like a boy, instead of a man of responsibilities. You need an heir."

Beresford narrowed his eyes at his mother, knowing that if he frowned a certain way, he reminded her of his father: authoritative, stern. Not to be ordered about. "If I am a man, then stop lecturing me like a child."

The countess sighed and tried another tack. "Do you not miss your friends? I imagine they are all heading to London for the start of the Season."

Beresford did wish some of his London friends would join him in Devon. He much preferred sailing or swimming to dancing. Alas, his friends were drawn by the lure of pretty females in the metropolis, and the promise of horse races, gambling, and theatre.

"I have friends here."

"Yes, common fishermen and village people. Isn't your fellow, Polkins, about to be married soon? You should take a leaf out of his book."

This, unfortunately, was true. Beresford's right-hand man, the lieutenant to his captain on his precious *Crescent*, had fallen in love with a village lass. Polkins was to be married in a week and was much preoccupied, leaving Beresford with a reduced crew and without a confidante. With Polkins about to be leg-shackled, it didn't seem right to grumble to him about the female half of the species.

The countess continued, folding her elegant hands in her lap. The matter of Beresford's marriage must really weigh on her if she had forgotten her cream tea. "Is there *any* appropriate girl you have taken a liking to? Out of all of England's finest you met in London last year?"

Beresford took a large bite of chudleigh and refused to comment. Briefly, however, an image of Miss Avely rose in his mind. Her curious hazel eyes and quick smile; her honey-coloured hair; her bold remarks and innocent demeanour. She was ... entertaining. That was all. Not enough to give up his bachelordom. He certainly wasn't going to mention Miss

Avely to his mother, who would promptly write to half of London to find out all she could about the poor girl.

"There must be at least *one*," pressed the countess, raising an inquisitive eyebrow.

"Not one," Beresford said shortly and licked the cream off his lips.

His mother eyed him speculatively and wisely changed the subject.

Later, Beresford escaped to the sea. He took his rowboat alone so he could be morose in private. If Polkins was obsessed over some chit, far be it for Beresford to glower over his wedding plans. Better to commune with the waves and catch some fish.

The sky was overcast and the waters calm: a lovely mid-spring day. Why on earth would one go to London now? Beresford weighed his anchor in a spot known for large whiting and settled in. His eyes travelled over the rocky coast. There were precious few nooks and crannies he didn't already know. He had explored this stretch of coast since he was a boy. Only more recently he had pressed further afield, as far as a sailing ship would take him: to France and back. Beresford yearned to go again, but he wouldn't be able to until he found another crewmate, one he could trust with his life. The French coast was dangerous, and not just because of the sea. The waters were rife with Napoleon's growing navy, and Beresford's trips were delicate endeavours.

A faint splash from behind the boat caught his attention. He turned and saw nothing except the water rippling. A fish jumping? A shadow moved below. A seal perhaps, or a dolphin. He saw plenty of both in his travels. Watching the quick movement, he leaned forward, hoping it would surface again. Sometimes the seals seemed almost human, with their large intelligent eyes and their way of frolicking about. Dolphins too, were playful, but somehow more detached.

It was a seal, he was certain. Beresford leaned a little closer, the fishing line loose in his hand. Way below, the figure seemed to squirm. Hurt? Or hunting?

Beresford put down his fishing line and peered over the edge of the boat.

A girl's face popped up out of the waves, and Beresford almost fell into the water.

"Good Gad!" he shouted, lurching backwards.

"How do you do?" said the girl. She had long, black hair and thick eyelashes. She was very pretty, with high cheekbones, full lips, and dark eyes. She was also naked, her only adornment a silver star shining in her hair. Her plump white arms lazily circled in the water, with her other attributes all too apparent in the clear sea.

Beresford clutched at the wooden seat and cleared

his throat. "I would not have moored my boat here if I knew it was a bathing place."

"Do not concern yourself," said the girl. She examined him with more curiosity than admiration. "Are you the Earl of Beresford?"

"I am." As if she did not know it. Beresford began to suspect she was out to entrap him; even he knew he was a very eligible bachelor. Perhaps she had even been sent by his mother. "I will leave you to your ablutions." He reached to haul up the anchor. He certainly didn't want to hang around naked, pretty village girls. He'd end up like Polkins.

"Please don't go." Her voice had a light timbre.

Beresford's hands stilled on the rope. The girl's accent was not common. In fact, she almost sounded like French nobility, but not quite that either. Beresford turned to examine her afresh.

Her eyes widened in entreaty. "Please, I am here to ask for your help."

"Who are you?"

"I am a selkie."

Beresford laughed. "Not a mermaid?" He had heard tales of selkies: the seal people who could take the form of both human and seal. Polkins used to entertain the crew with various stories, including those of mermaids, faeries, and selkies. Children's stories.

The girl batted her long eyelashes, drops sparkling at the tips. "Oh, no. Mermaids are far prettier."

He refused to take the bait. In his opinion, she was too young to be flirting like that. "Are they now? And I suppose you can turn into a seal in a blink?"

With an arch smile, she blinked slowly, shuttering her long lashes and then widening her eyes. Beresford smiled despite himself, to see her theatrics. Then she slipped under the water and turned into a seal.

It was done within a minute, amid the waves swirling. The white flesh vanished, and in its place, a brown velvet head emerged. The seal looked at Beresford and blinked her dark eyes again, in a mimicry of her human action. The silver star, still clinging to her temple somehow, removed any remaining doubt that it was she.

Beresford did not allow his mouth to gape. He was far too well-trained as a peer of the realm to permit such uncouth behaviour. But his breath drew in sharply, and he was aware of his heartbeat thudding in his ears.

He stared for a long moment, speechless. So Polkins had been telling the truth in his tales, possibly unbeknownst even to himself.

The seal barked at him. It was a light yap, but it snapped Beresford out of his disbelief.

"Very well. I believe you. Turn human again, for heaven's sake."

She did so with a flick of a brown tail. Once again, a lovely girl smirked up at him from the water.

"Good Gad," said Beresford again.

"Now, will you help me?"

"Why should I help you?" He tried to remember the tales from Polkins. Was it bad luck to refuse aid to a selkie? Or was it madness if he *did* help her?

"My brother is missing."

"Your brother?" For some reason, this was the final straw. Beresford began to laugh. "You have a brother, like yourself?"

"Of course." She frowned at him. "I do not see why that is amusing. He looks very similar to me; everyone says so." Her expression darkened. "Though he is *not* as beautiful as me."

Beresford raised a brow, but she continued, still frowning. "Two days ago, my brother vanished. I need your help to find him."

Beresford sobered. "Why me?"

The girl gave him a limpid look. "You are a man. A handsome, capable man. And an earl."

He narrowed his eyes. He knew very well he wasn't handsome. Striking, perhaps, in a certain light, and especially when holding a jar of the Beresford Plum Jam. Ladies always flocked to the jam. This young selkie, however, didn't know of the jam. Or did she?

As for capable, he was that. And an earl, accustomed to authority. Beresford applied his wits. "If you have a brother, you must have a father."

"My family is already looking. My *mother* has all her men searching the seas. Of course, she would send all her resources after him: Jaq is her favourite."

"So why have you come to me?" Beresford repeated the question.

The girl flicked her black hair over her shoulder, impatiently. "You can search on land, my lord. You might have seen something or know something. You have power, influence, and certain *connections*." He wondered exactly what she meant by that; then, she changed her frown to a twinkle. "And lovely broad shoulders."

He really ought to tell her that he preferred blondes, if only to put her off. And Miss Avely *was* blonde, with lovely honey-colored hair. For a moment he wondered what Miss Avely would say if confronted with this outrageous, impossible creature. No doubt she would take it in her stride: calm, curious, and eager to know more. Well, so would he.

"Would your brother survive long on land?"

"Long enough, if not in the best of health. Also, he might not be very well ... equipped."

Beresford eyed her. "You mean he might be ... unclothed?"

She nodded. "And possibly drunk."

"Well, I am certain the news will travel fast if he is sighted on land," said Beresford dryly. "Why can't you go to the village yourself, to find out if anyone has mentioned him?" Even as he said it, he realised this was probably unwise.

"Mother will not let me go on land. There is a risk we would give ourselves away if any selkie folk go ashore."

That would certainly be true if she waltzed into the local inn in her current state of undress.

"Does your mother know you are talking to me?"

Her gaze slid out to the horizon. "No."

"How old are you?"

She straightened her shoulders, which had the unfortunate effect of lifting her upper body slightly out of the water. Beresford averted his eyes.

"I am twenty-one. My birthday was two days ago," she said proudly. "My name is Seraphine."

"I begin to comprehend, Miss Seraphine." Beresford made his tone authoritative. "You are not in your parents' power anymore. And you have sneaked off to do the very things you are not supposed to do. Luckily for you, I am an honourable man and will not speak of this to anyone. Now go home, and trust the matter to your elders."

The girl looked scornful. "Who cares if I am here without permission! A man's life is in the balance! My brother could die, my lord, and you are too scared to help."

"Nonsense. Your brother is probably off on a lark – waylaying a human, just like you."

"My lord, he has been taken hostage," said Seraphine coldly. "He is being held for ransom. And he might die."

CHAPTER 3

Jaq

Far away, Jaq felt as if he might actually die. His head throbbed, his body ached, and to cap it all off, he was tied to a boulder, naked and thirsty.

"Fenner!" he called. "Give a man a drink! Just water."

There was a splash, and a different merman swam through the underwater tunnel which joined the two caves. A blue head emerged near Jaq's feet, and he recognised Costo's face grinning at him. Like all merpeople, Costo's eyes were mostly pupil, black and opaque like those of a fish. It was slightly unnerving when one first met them, but Jaq was used to it.

However, Costo's gaze was particularly inscrutable: he was the head of this little cohort of mermen and known for his cool head in a gamble.

Costo crossed his blue arms over the rock and stared unblinkingly at Jaq. "A bit below standard, are you?"

"Pretty awful."

"Coral cutthroat will do that."

"I didn't think I had so much." Jaq would still swear he only had three cups. Not enough, surely, to feel like this.

"It happens," said Costo, dryly.

Jaq shifted. "Now, Costo, I want to know the details. What have you done?"

The merman chuckled. "I sent off a polite little note to your mother, asking for two thousand guineas."

Jaq almost fell over himself, only he was already on the ground. "*Two thousand guineas?* Are you mad? She'll never pay that."

"So humble, Your Majesty."

"I'm going to die," Jaq groaned.

"We won't kill you, little cub. Not yet."

"My *mother* is going to kill me."

"Well, you are safe from her here."

"She'll have everyone searching."

"We're tucked away, don't you worry." Costo tossed him a flask. "Here."

Jaq took a swig, then gagged. "I said water!"

"Fenner!" Costo yelled. "Bring his highness some freshwater. He might die otherwise."

"You don't want that," pointed out Jaq. "You will lose your best card."

Costo gave him an enigmatic look, and Jaq felt a shiver run over his skin. He had known Costo for at least a year. The merman was cruel in a way typical to his species, but Jaq didn't think Costo would actually harm him. Would he? Surely not, if there were two thousand guineas in the balance.

After a long drink of freshwater, Jaq felt slightly better. The mermen left him – they were in the middle of a game of craken – and Jaq was alone with his thoughts. Unfortunately, these were gaining in clarity.

Hazy memories of Seraphine's birthday now surfaced. He had been inexcusably, disgustingly, terribly, drunk. Something had happened on the way to the ceremony – something involving Seraphine. She had been furious with him, that much was certain. He remembered her dark eyes flashing with anger and distress, her voice loud and shouting.

It didn't add up. He would swear on his mother's crown that he hadn't drunk that much. Someone must have slipped him something extra. The way Jaq felt now, it was probably mermaid tears. Combined with the celebratory skerrysun and three cups of coral cutthroat, the mix would explain his previous bad behaviour and current mortification.

It must have been Costo. Curse the fish. Though why Costo felt he needed to add tears to the mix, Jaq did not know. He had arranged to meet the mermen himself after Seraphine's party anyway, and he would have gone along willingly enough to this cave. Why did they have to ruin his sister's birthday by mixing his drinks?

Of course, it was Jaq who had ruined Seraphine's birthday.

He groaned and dropped his head back against the cold stone.

CHAPTER 4

Beresford

The next time Beresford saw Seraphine, he was walking along a bay further south of where he had been fishing. Despite her protestations, he had sent her away, but the following morning he looked up to see her strolling towards him along the beach. It was a windy day, with only flashes of sunlight catching on the water, yet Seraphine was completely naked again.

Beresford supposed that her seal nature gave her additional protection against the cold. However, to add insult to injury, she was undulating her hips in a completely ridiculous manner.

"Oh, for Lord's sake!" He took off his jacket and hurried towards her. "What are you doing? Put this on."

Seraphine looked pleased. "So you are prudish! They told me humans are."

"If you mean we prefer to be dressed, then yes!"

"Especially the English," she observed, as her black hair tossed in the wind. "Selkies do not mind about such matters. I wanted to see how you would react." She put the jacket on, fingering the material dubiously and, as an afterthought, gave him a saucy smile. The silver star glinted at her temple as before.

"I am not your little experiment," objected Beresford, though he rather thought he was. "You ought not to be on land."

"In a crisis, the usual rules are laid aside," Seraphine said regally.

"Does that mean you have permission to be here now?"

"Not exactly." She took on a defiant air. "I am of age now."

"Your brother is still missing?"

"It has been three days now." Seraphine pulled the coat closer around her shoulders. "You must help."

"I must not do anything." Beresford did not want to admit he had already been looking, a little. There was no gossip in the local inn about any drunk, naked boy wandering around the coast. One hoped there would not be any about Seraphine either.

She frowned at him. "I will keep finding you until you do." She paused. "I know where you live."

"Good Gad." He imagined her coming naked to the manor: his mother's face, and his butler's. "You would not dare."

"I would."

Beresford took her arm, then realised he didn't know where to escort her. But she looked pleased and began strolling along the sand as if she were at Hyde Park, showing off a suitor. Damnable females. They were the same everywhere.

"Are you certain your brother has been taken hostage?" he asked, as the question had been bothering him.

"Yes, we had the note the morning after he vanished."

"Your family could simply pay the ransom."

Seraphine shot him a scornful look. "Would you?"

Beresford sighed and shook his head slightly.

"No, you would try to find him first. Furthermore, the note asked for two thousand guineas."

"Two thousand guineas?" Beresford bit his lip to refrain from uttering an obscenity before a lady. "That's a lot of money, enough to buy a house in London." He turned to look at Seraphine more closely. "Who is your brother? Who are you?"

She fluttered her eyelashes. "I forgot to mention – my mother is the Queen of Skerry."

Again, years of training kept Beresford's gait steady, and his gaze calm. "Oh? You are a princess?"

Seraphine dipped her head. "Indeed. My brother is the High Prince of Skerry."

Beresford considered her in a new light. No wonder she thought she could do as she liked and assumed that all men would bow down to her will. He decided not to give her any more satisfaction and kept walking, ostensibly unfazed by the royal title.

"Honoured, I am sure," he said dryly. "Is your brother like you, overly curious about humans?"

Seraphine nodded, sashaying along, sublimely oblivious of Beresford's tone of reproof. "Jaq is a packet of trouble. It is completely unsurprising to me that he has been taken hostage."

"Oh?"

"He is always drinking, gambling, and swimming with the wrong crowd. He might have put his head above water in the wrong place and been snatched by land folk. Or he might be with the merfolk. He was dallying with a group called the Wastrels – trouble, all of them." She frowned. "If the mermen have taken him, it is even more worrisome, as it will cause trouble between the merfolk and my people. The Mer-Selkie treaties may come apart. You wouldn't want that, as human ships will be attacked more often by the merfolk."

"You are telling me mermaids are involved?" Beresford suspected she might be pulling his leg, and he frowned at her.

She didn't see his expression. "Possibly. Or perhaps Jaq just had far too much to drink – a not unknown occurrence – and managed to hurt himself. And then some criminal saw it as an opportunity."

Seraphine's voice quivered. It was the first sign of real distress she had shown. Beresford flashed her a glance. Her beautiful profile stared straight ahead, with her chin tilted at a proud angle.

The wind blew a black lock across her face, and waves rolled with a hiss onto the sand beside them. Beresford sought for something reassuring to say. "Surely, the hostage note would mention if Jaq were injured."

"I suppose so." She turned, and her eyes were even more liquid than usual, perhaps with tears. "The last time I saw Jaq, we had a terrible fight. I was furious with him. And now he is gone. What if I never get a chance to say I'm sorry for all the dreadful things I said?"

Beresford nodded with sudden decision. "I will try to find your brother." Seraphine's brows lifted in sudden excitement, transforming her expression, and he felt a flash of doubt. "I will use my ship to search the coastline." It was a good excuse to take to the sea; he would tell his mother he was going on a fishing trip.

Seraphine gripped his arm tightly. "Oh, I thank you!"

He sighed. "Just promise me you will refrain from visiting my house."

CHAPTER 5

Jaq

On the fateful day of Seraphine's birthday party, Jaq had arrived at his sister's quarters early for once, or so it seemed. Seraphine, like Jaq, had her own set of land rooms in the Imravoe Palace, though hers were at the front of that granite and limestone sprawl. Her balcony had a stunning view, as Imravoe was located on the biggest isle of Skerry and looked over the whole circle of islands, including the rolling vineyards. But it was also the least private balcony, and already selkies were gathering below in anticipation of Seraphine's appearance.

Jaq was there to escort her to the ceremony, but Seraphine's boudoir was empty. Only piles of silks, flowers, and presents met his eye, some gifts still unopened. Her dressing table was laden with bottles, creams, and bouquets, and her chair was pushed in. Even Seraphine's servants weren't there, which was odd. Perhaps they were looking for her. They would be anxious to dress her.

Jaq threw himself on a settee and waited. He was in fine fettle, slightly and delightfully inebriated on skerrysun. The day was glorious. Sunlight streamed in from the balcony window, setting the silks alight. He gazed around, dreamily running his fingers over a particularly soft lace. Perhaps he was a bit more than *slightly* inebriated. The tiara on Seraphine's dressing table sparkled in a most fascinating manner.

Outside the window, Jaq could see the soft undulations of the other green isles of Skerry. Low limestone buildings gleamed in the sun, tucked into the circling dunes, but the grandest were saved for Imravoe. High Skerry even sported cobblestone streets and carriages imported from France. That was more for show; selkies didn't need too many land comforts. They were just as happy in the sea.

Jaq ran a thumb over a ruffle of feathers, taken from the golden crest of a gannet. He marvelled at the softness: they were so fine he could barely feel them. Only later did he realise that it must have been the mermaid tears that had heightened his senses so.

Combined with skerrysun, he had been as high as a kestrel that day, ecstatic at every tiny thing.

Only after half an hour of blissfully rifling through Seraphine's birthday gifts did Jaq have a faint sense of worry. Where was his sister? She ought to be here by now, preparing for the ceremony. Jaq hummed a tune, smiling at himself in the mirror. He, too, was dressed in his finest: land garb, with breeches and tailcoat, but a royal touch in the gold lace cloak thrown over the top. He did look the spitting image of his sister, though a bit more manly, he fancied.

Heaven forbid Seraphine turn up at the ceremony as a seal, in her silver lace alone. Jaq hoped that *she* had not partaken too liberally of skerrysun and forgotten her duties. It was easy to do. He knew from experience.

He frowned, hearing the crowd gathering outside. They, also, were waiting to escort their princess. It was tradition that she wave from the balcony before journeying to the sanctuary, surrounded by her loyal subjects.

It sounded as though the crowd was becoming impatient. Looking at the clock above the door, Jaq realised with a sense of surprise that he had been waiting an hour. Seraphine was rather late indeed.

He grimaced, thinking of what his mother would say if she heard Seraphine had neglected her obligations. Poor Seraph, to be raked over the reef on the day of her birthday. Jaq stared out the window, feeling quite sorry for her, even though it was hard to feel much concern with skerrysun coursing through him.

He couldn't quite pinpoint when the idea came to him. Perhaps it was because he already had a silver lace cloak at his elbow, and it was a simple matter to throw off his gold one. He tucked the silver one over himself and sat down at the dressing table.

Where were servants when you needed them? He would have to do his own hair. Jaq set about untying it from its gold riband and curled it down around his face, placing a few jewels artlessly in his black locks. Better hide his Age Star – Seraphine would not have hers until the end of the day, so he made sure his own was hidden under the curls at the back of his head. His eyebrows were a bit heavy, but no one would remark that from the courtyard below.

Carefully, Jaq applied a little rouge and cream, whistling to himself. The cream was so creamy! Perhaps a little extra. The tiara would look very well on his head. Jaq examined his reflection, grinning. Everyone always said he and Seraphine were almost identical. If he pouted a little, he certainly could be taken for her, especially if he added a little colour to his lips and stuck his nose in the air.

He soon fixed the matter of his breeches by pulling on a lovely skirt, the colour of the sky on a summer's day. It was long enough to hide his boots too, and a marvellous texture, like sunlight sliding through his fingers. His coat was dealt with by the expedient of choosing the biggest bouquet of flowers and holding it in front of him, where the silver lace parted. There, that would serve. The flowers smelled divine.

He winked at the mirror, very pleased with himself, and then stepped out onto the balcony.

A roar of approval rose up to meet him. The crowd was larger now, teeming on the paved courtyard: a mass of selkie faces with more in the sea behind. Even the merpeople were there, some as a reluctant concession to the treaties, but others just for a good time.

Petals and starflowers flew up, fluttering in the air around him. Jaq raised a hand and waved graciously. Another cheer arose.

He smiled, remembering this moment of adulation from his own Age Day. Only he hadn't worn so many jewels then. He tossed his head so they sparkled in the sun and then sashayed across the balcony, blowing kisses.

He made sure to pout.

Hundreds of adoring faces looked up at him.

"Princess!" cried one.

"Our princess! Happy Age Day!" cried another. A rose landed at Jaq's feet: a gracious tribute, as roses were difficult to acquire in Skerry.

He grinned. It was working.

Nodding regally, he bent to pick up the bloom,

careful not to expose his coat. He clutched the bouquet and the rose, smiling around, victorious. Handkerchiefs and flowers waved up at him.

It was all going so well, and he was having such a good time. Then on his tenth lap of the balcony – just as he did a little twirl – a carriage rolled up behind the crowd.

It was an open carriage with the royal crest. Sitting upon it, clothed in royal splendour, was Seraphine.

She, also, was waving graciously.

Jaq met her gaze, and for a long terrible moment they both froze, hands aloft in a dreadful mirror image. Only, thought Jaq, his skirt was a nicer colour.

The crowd turned to see what the royal eyes had fixed upon.

There was sudden silence. A hundred heads swung back and forth, trying to make sense of the double vision. Then a titter rustled, gaining in volume, rippling and rolling like waves until it reached full tide.

Jaq laughed, too, for the joke was infectious, especially when one's sense of humour was augmented by skerrysun. He continued to wave even as Seraphine's hand dropped. He dipped a deep curtsy, grinning.

The crowd roared their approval again. Jaq pouted once more for good measure and threw his bouquet with a grand gesture into the masses. Might as well carry the thing off properly. He flicked his hair and blew one last kiss.

Making his exit, he glanced at Seraphine. Her face was white, and her smile was forced. But as the crowd turned to her, wiping their eyes, Seraphine lifted her head high and stood in the carriage to address them.

Back inside the boudoir, Jaq hastily stripped off the skirt and tiara. Hurriedly, he put the jewels back and removed the colours from his face. He now had to join Seraphine in the carriage, as tradition required. Grimacing to himself, he made his way down to board the carriage, clothed in his gold cloak once more.

The crowd parted with a cheer of appreciation as he passed through.

Seraphine gave him a glare: it would have felled a man less under the influence of skerrysun. Jaq smiled widely and leapt onto the step.

"You damned eel," said Seraphine through gritted teeth, also smiling widely. "You ... preening popinjay!"

He winked at her. "Pretty though. Like you."

His attempt at flattery did not work.

"Sit down," she ground out. "Not another word."

They both knew better than to present anything other than a united front. So Jaq sat demurely at her side for the remainder of the short journey, both of them nodding, smiling, and waving.

The damage, however, was done. News of his escapade spread quickly, and everywhere he looked, there were grinning faces, catcalls, and teasing remarks. "There go two princesses," called one appreciative subject. "Your Highness, you're looking lovely today," called another, and everyone knew he was referring to Jaq.

Seraphine was red with mortification and fury, though it simply gave her cheeks a becoming flush. "Wait until Mother hears about this," she hissed under her breath, waving prettily. "She will have plenty to say, I am certain."

These dire words had wiped the smile off Jaq's face. Even skerrysun couldn't completely lighten the august and icy vision of his mother's disapproval when she heard about this latest antic. Mother would not appreciate the fact he had only been trying to help and furthermore had chosen a better dress than Seraphine.

However, his mother had not spoken to him later. She hadn't had the chance.

Seraphine had said more than enough. She had screamed at Jaq after the ceremony, called him every name under the sea. Jaq had been surprised at her vocabulary and asked where Seraphine had learned such things. She had stomped her foot, shaken her fist at him, and told him not to be such pestilence of sea slugs. Starting to come down from his high, Jaq had shouted back. After a fight of royal proportions, he had stormed off to find the mermen.

He had woken to find himself here.

At least it was a small respite. At least Jaq's head had stopped hurting.

The game was desultory. Jaq was now in the deeper cave, lying on another slab of rock with his ankles still tied. The rope led to a boulder below the water, but now he held his own set of coral cards. Fortunately, he had also been fed – not royally, but at least with fish. His head was starting to clear, and he was winning the game, though Jaq doubted it would do much to recover the huge amount he already owed the Wastrels from his spectacularly bad dolphin race two weeks ago.

He wondered, idly, if he ought to try escaping. His mother would be worried. It was probably good for her to worry a bit. Still, he had been in this godforsaken mercave for three days now. And the payment still might arrive.

A bitter thought occurred to Jaq: if it hadn't been for the ransom note, no one would have even noticed he was gone. Seraphine was probably *glad* he was gone.

"Seven," Jaq said with satisfaction, putting down a card.

Fenner wrinkled his nose. "Two."

Costo scowled and tossed down a ten.

Swordfish was difficult to learn, but Jaq had played

it since he was a pup, and he wasn't currently drunk. "Ace."

Costo threw his cards down in disgust. "You have Triton's own luck, Your Majesty."

"Amphitrite's luck. And stop calling me that," Jaq leaned back. "I thought we were friends."

Orrow, a merman with very dark green skin, had been watching the play. He chuckled. "You're the best kind of friend. You're netting us a fortune."

"Then stop mocking my title. You know I don't want to be a prince." Jaq gathered in his winnings. "My sister will inherit the crown anyway."

Costo raised his brows. "Seraphine is younger than you. I'm still of the opinion that you ought to be the heir apparent."

Jaq repressed a stab of anger at the informal use of his sister's name. "The High Princess, however, is female."

"Ah," said Fenner. "It's true you don't have … attributes … like Seraphine."

Jaq started to his feet, ignoring the rope and the fact that his blanket fell to the ground. "Do not talk about my sister like that!"

Fenner raised his hands. "Sorry, *Your Nakedness*."

Jaq scowled at him.

Costo also frowned at Fenner. "There will be no more references to her Royal Highness's more …

delightful aspects." Jaq took a threatening step towards Costo, and the rope pulled at his ankle. Costo smiled and shook his head. "Unless it is Seraphine's riches. Perhaps we should have ransomed the High Princess instead."

Jaq sank back onto the rock and pulled the blanket back over him. "You would not dare." It was one thing to take a disposable brother, but to take the heir apparent would pull down the wrath of his mother for certain.

"We have no need," replied Costo. "We have you. Even if you are not next in line for the throne, you're still the darling of your mother's heart."

"So you think." After the debacle of Seraphine's birthday, Jaq's name was more likely uttered as a curse than in fondness. He turned to Costo, tossing down his next card. "Did you put tears in my drink on my sister's Age Day?"

Costo flicked his tail in the water, watching the luminescent drops scatter. "Tears? No. Did you ask for some? Looked to me as if you were having a pleasant enough time without them."

"I did not ask," said Jaq. "Yet some were in my drink."

"Why do you say that?" Costo raised his brows.

"Look what happened! Did you see what happened?"

"Oh yes," said Orrow, grinning. "Everyone saw. Beautiful, you were."

Jaq gave a wry twist of his lips. "Thank you. But Skerrysun wouldn't make me behave like that. Not by itself. Not on my sister's birthday, at Imravoe."

Costo flicked his tail again, contemptuously. "You are quite capable of ridiculous behaviour without blaming it on tears."

Jaq frowned at him. "But you put some in my drink, didn't you?"

Though why would Costo do that if he already had Jaq's co-operation? There was also the irksome matter of the rope around Jaq's ankles and the odd look Costo had given him in the inner cave. Did the merman have some larger plan, even more ambitious than ransom?

For the first time, Jaq wondered if it was Costo's plan to destabilise the Mer-Selkie treaties. Costo had always spoken against the alliance, but Jaq thought it had been mere posturing: drunken angry rants. However, the audacious capture of a prince would certainly twitch some whiskers – especially if said prince was harmed or killed. Jaq narrowed his eyes at the leader of the Wastrels.

Costo stared back. "It was not I," he said shortly. "I had no reason to do such a thing."

Jaq dropped his own gaze. It was a silly thought; of course, Costo had no reason. They had raced together, and it would be dishonourable to betray a fellow gambler like that.

Fenner shook his head. "Wasn't us. Might have been someone else, though. It's true you seemed a bit ... wailed."

Jaq sighed. He had been overcome by silks and feathers. It must have been tears.

Who, then, had put them in his drink?

CHAPTER 6

Beresford

At the helm of his schooner, Beresford felt the wind in his face and smiled. He was out at sea again, with his usual crew of Allen and Kendall, sturdy, dependable village lads who knew how to keep their mouths shut. Even Polkins had agreed to join him, despite the lieutenant's wedding being only five days away.

Beresford had not told his men what he was searching for at sea. They were used to his covert quests, and they knew not to ask too many questions. Thank goodness for that, for Beresford scarcely knew how to explain Seraphine.

It turned out he didn't have to explain. She showed

up in the water, an hour out of Deockley, just as Beresford half expected she would.

Allen and Kendall had eyes like saucers and mouths like plates. Polkins, the good man, managed to keep a cool head and announced calmly to his captain that there was a woman overboard.

"I can see that," said Beresford, peering into the surging, green waves. Seraphine was floating like a painting on the surface, black hair coiling and white limbs apparent enough to convince anyone she was not a mermaid. She seemed to be clad in a white, lacy cloak that did nothing to obscure anything.

"Ahoy!" called Seraphine. "Good afternoon, gentlemen! May I come aboard your vessel?" She gave a dazzling smile, and the star in her hair flashed.

"Turn your gaze away," Beresford commanded his men. They promptly turned to starboard, and he heaved a rope over the port side. "What the devil are you doing, Seraphine?"

He belated realised that this was an improper way to speak to a lady. However, it was certainly better to leave the royal title out of it for the moment. A naked woman was bad enough; a naked princess might tip the men over the edge.

"Assisting the venture, of course," said Seraphine, pulling herself up the rope with surprising strength. The lace garment clung to her body, the white contrasting with her dark hair. "I have a right. Jaq is my brother, after all."

"Into the cabin," Beresford ordered. "You'll find clothes there."

"I am wearing clothes." Seraphine stepped onto the deck and flicked out her cloak.

"*That* does not count." He could sense his men were dying to turn around, with their fidgeting and shifting. "As I said, clothes await you in the cabin." Beresford had possessed enough foresight to have smuggled lady's attire onto the ship – one of his mother's old gowns, from before the countess went into mourning. It was old-fashioned, striped calico, too big for Seraphine (who really was quite short), but it would serve.

Offended, Seraphine stalked across to the cabin, scattering water and slamming the door behind her voluptuous form. In the ensuing silence, Beresford briefly explained that Seraphine's brother was missing at sea, and they were not to talk of this to anyone.

Kendall and Allen shook their heads mutely. Polkins ventured a question. "Is she a selkie, then?"

Beresford turned on him. "I thought they were just tales," he snapped. "You should have warned me they were true."

"I thought I did," said Polkins slowly. "Though, to be honest, I didn't know for certain."

"Fine-looking lass," put in Allen, in reverent tones.

"Not my type," said Beresford shortly. Everyone looked at him askance.

Kendall's eyes were still round. "Is she really a selkie?"

The cabin door swung open. Seraphine stood clad in the striped gown, holding the skirts in her hand. Beresford breathed a sigh of relief to see she was properly covered.

"I am indeed a selkie," she announced, in a grand manner. "Noble gentlemen, I thank you for your assistance. It is prodigious good luck to help selkies. Now, where shall we look first?"

They headed to the far south of Devon, for that was the most lonesome part of the coast. Beresford suspected Seraphine's pesky brother might have run into trouble there, either on the treacherous rocks or with a surly fisherman. Polkins said he had heard tell of fishermen capturing selkies, though he hadn't believed it possible until now. Beresford suggested that it would be hard to find a fisherman with enough gumption to write a ransom note to a selkie queen.

Seraphine agreed. "That is why I think it is the mermen. A human would not know Jaq was a prince. Though Jaq may have announced it, I suppose."

Beresford frowned. "Would the mermen dare take a prince hostage?"

"They might, for the money. The merfolk cannot go on land; they are dependent on selkie trade. Or anything they lure from humans."

"You mean a shipwreck?"

Seraphine nodded, folding her hands in her lap, enjoying the attention, but she looked even more like a child in the oversized gown. "Merlures. They sing the ships in, take everything. Cold-hearted folk, the merfolk. Closer to fish than to men."

The waves lurched around them, slate grey, and a seagull gave a mournful cry.

"Cold-hearted enough to take a boy hostage, then," said Beresford.

Seraphine raised a brow. "I never said Jaq was a boy."

"Oh. How old is he?"

"Twenty-three. Though that is about forty-six of your human years."

Beresford digested this. "So he is only two years older than you. Like I said: a boy."

Seraphine stuck her chin in the air. "I am a woman now." A hand crept up to her hair, where the silver star shone. "I have my Star now."

Beresford did not give her the satisfaction of asking what it signified. "And where do the merfolk spend their time?"

"Deep in the seas," said Polkins, coming up next to Seraphine. "We can't find merfolk."

"They also like caves and lagoons," argued Seraphine. "If they have Jaq, they will be somewhere ashore, where he can breathe."

So they searched. Beresford knew many of the caves along the south of England; it was his job to know such things. He had to admit Seraphine had come to the right person and wondered how much she and her people knew about him.

After a day's hard sailing and searching, they had nothing to show for it. The coast was desolate and empty, and anyone they saw denied any knowledge of a handsome boy with dark hair who might have found himself in trouble.

At last, it was time to drop anchor and settle for the night. Seraphine was determined to stay with them, despite the impropriety of being alone on a ship with a crew of men. She took great enjoyment in the simple supper, and climbed eagerly into the cabin bed, snuggling into the woollen blankets.

Beresford sighed as he shut the door. He would be sleeping in a hammock tonight – like the rest of his crew.

The next day, Seraphine announced that she had decided they should talk to the merfolk directly.

"*Talk* to them?" asked Beresford. "You think the merfolk will just tell us where your brother is?"

"Yes, if it were the Wastrels who took him. Others might be willing to help or tell us where the Wastrels are."

"Remind me, who are the Wastrels?"

"That group of good-for-nothing mermen I mentioned. They like drinking and gambling – so Jaq likes them. He spends too much time in their company, and they might have seen it as an opportunity. They were always eyeing him up."

Beresford raised his brows but decided he did not want to ask about that.

Polkins looked awed. "How do we parley with merfolk?"

"We go to their lagoon," said Seraphine. "I will show you the way."

"No," said Beresford.

"Why ever not?"

"You don't trust the merfolk. Why would you waltz up to them like that?"

Seraphine blinked. "They would not harm *me*."

"They've taken your brother hostage!"

"Oh, but I'm heir to the throne. The merfolk wouldn't go so far as to endanger *me*."

Beresford was confused. "I thought you said Jaq is older than you? Is he not in line for the throne?"

"We are a matriarchy," explained Seraphine. "I do not expect you barbaric Englishmen to understand, but the crown passes to a woman. Jaq will only ever be a High Prince, while I will be Queen one day." She smoothed her calico skirts and tilted her head, glinting at Beresford. "As you see."

He raised a brow. "You are no queen, miss."

"Not yet. But I am perfectly able to parley with mermaids. Now, take me to the lagoon. It is quite near here. And depending on what they tell me, you may still prove useful."

Beresford sighed. He supposed he was in too deep now. Chivalry demanded that he assist Seraphine in her quest, and besides, he *was* rather curious to see a mermaid haunt.

The lagoon was hidden in a rocky isle out in the middle of the ocean. It took them three hours to find it, and by then, Beresford was rather surly. Seraphine, sitting on the quarterdeck and fanning herself in the sun, seemed to think her duty consisted entirely of looking pretty. To be fair, he didn't want her helping to sail the ship. She had already tried that and almost killed Kendall.

"Ah!" she shouted. "I see the white lichen-stars. Throw your anchor in, men!"

"I am the captain," said Beresford. "I'll give the orders." He paused. "Throw in the anchor, Polkins. We need to rest if nothing else."

He considered the stretch of rock: it did not look promising, though small sandy dunes obscured his view of the whole. At least the day was clear, and the waters calm and blue.

Seraphine stood on the quarterdeck and began taking off her clothes.

"Good Gad, Seraphine, have you no sense of decorum?" shouted Beresford, seeing his men transfixed.

Her hands stilled at the ties. "I am going to swim in as a seal. You do not want me to soak the gown, do you?"

"Change your gown in the cabin. At least put on that flimsy white fabric." He did not want to grace it with the name of 'cloak.'

She shrugged. "I am sure your men can handle the sight of me jumping into the water."

Looking at Allen and Kendall, whose features once again resembled crockery, Beresford doubted it. "And put a blanket over the top, for Lord's sake. We can dry it out later. And crew, turn your gaze to port!"

With something less than alacrity, his men turned to stare out over the portside surging waves, their backs now to the selkie princess.

Rolling her eyes, Seraphim fetched an old red blanket. Then she stalked across the deck and jumped into the ocean. The blanket billowed momentarily, and a brown shape surfaced beside it, still somehow clad in lace. Seraphine winked at Beresford with a dark seal eye, and then dipped and dove away from the ship.

"Damn it," swore Beresford, and he stripped off to dive in after the blanket.

When Seraphine returned an hour later, he and the blanket were drying out on the deck, and Beresford was extremely irate. "Well? What did the mermaids say?"

Seraphine blinked the water out of her human eyes, treading water. "They want to meet you."

He narrowed his gaze. "Meet *me?*"

"Of course."

"Why?"

"I told them about you. They said they would tell all they know, on the proviso that they are permitted to meet a human earl. Oh, and I promised them some of that Beresford Plum Jam as a gift in return. Bring some in the rowboat."

"How do you know about the Beresford Jam?"

Seraphine blinked again. "Everyone knows about the Beresford Jam."

Beresford shrugged, admitting the truth of this, though he had not known the fame extended to mermaid territories. "I, however, do not know much about *you*. How can I know if you are trustworthy?"

Seraphine looked affronted, her arms moving more rapidly in the water. "I am the High Princess of Skerry!"

"Your whole story could be a lie, designed to lure me into a lagoon to be trapped by mermaids."

"Ah, is that what you wish?" She smirked, and behind Beresford, Kendall cleared his throat in embarrassment. "Unfortunately, there is no trap." Seraphine giggled, then paused. "There is one thing I can do to prove my good intentions."

"What is that?"

"I can give you my Star." She pointed to her hair, where it gleamed. "It would be a remarkable gesture of trust, as ordinarily, I would never give it to anyone."

At Beresford's sceptical expression, she explained. "If you have my Star, you have my co-operation – effectively, I am your vassal. I am bound to do as you say and to stay within its reach unless you give me permission to go further. I have only just received my Star from my mother, so it is very good of me to offer it to you." An uneasy look crossed Seraphine's face as she said it, and she reached to caress the star as if to reassure herself it was still there. "It would be a suitable sacrifice if you need it to trust our alliance."

"Oh, is that so?"

"You can test it if you like; I cannot lie to you while you hold it."

Beresford did not know whether to believe her, but when she sighed and reluctantly pulled the star from her hair and tossed it up to him, he was careful to catch it. Warm in his hands, it tingled slightly.

He decided to see if she would indeed speak the truth. "Tell me how you knew about me."

Seraphine flicked hair out of her eyes and frowned. "My mother's guard told me." She paused. "He has been told to watch you before."

"What does this guard know about me?"

She chewed her lip and cast a reluctant glance at the star in Beresford's hands. "He knows you work for your king. That you know the coastline well. That you travel to France. That is all." She cast a sidelong look at the men at his back.

Beresford let his hand drop. "Too much for my liking."

"I would have thought you would *want* to see a mermaid lagoon." Seraphine splashed a hand petulantly. "Most men would give a fortune to see it. Mermaids are very beautiful. Even more so than me."

"They can hardly be more vain," muttered Beresford.

Polkins spoke from behind him. "Do it, my lord, for all our sakes. It is an opportunity not to be missed. We'll come in after you if you don't come back."

"That is what I am concerned about," Beresford replied.

"I will protect you," said Seraphine.

"Obliged, I'm sure."

Seraphine frowned at him. "The mermaids won't cause any trouble. They just want to sample some plum jam, then they will be amenable to our questions."

Beresford sighed. "I am certain they will be. Very well, I will row us in."

"Oh no," she said. "We have to swim."

CHAPTER 7

Beresford

After swimming ashore and clambering over rocks and dunes (a task made more difficult by the fact that he was carrying a large jar of jam), Beresford found an indigo stretch of water shaped like a shell and sheltered from the sea winds. No trees grew on the barren stone, only lichen and small white flowers, five-petalled in the shape of stars. The still water lapped quietly, and grey seabirds picked their way through the rockpools.

In the shallows on the far side, several feminine shapes were half-submerged in the water. Their hands held something that looked like seaweed, and their strange eyes were turned towards him.

Seraphine, clad once more in the red blanket (which Beresford insisted she wear), led the way. Beresford followed, dripping wet in his plain white shirt and grey breeches. He certainly was not going to go into a mermaid's den unclothed, even if Seraphine suggested that was the best way to do it.

However, as the mermaids sized him up, it felt as if he *were* naked. There were nine mermaids, each exquisitely beautiful – if one liked blue or green hair and pale blue skin. Beresford decided he didn't. He still preferred Miss Avely. She, at least, wore proper clothing.

It looked as if the mermaids were weaving something out of seaweed, though it now lay lax in their hands at his approach. Beresford's sharp eyes saw a pile of baskets made from the same weed, stacked together neatly. Not such a fearsome activity then, and no human bones in sight, only collections of shells. The ladies' fishtails shimmered in the water, catching the sunlight.

"Good afternoon, my lord earl," said one, who appeared to be the leader. She was long in the body and teal-haired, with strange fisheyes. She stared at him unblinking. "You are a fine man."

"A bit more broad and hairy than our men," one remarked. "Still, I like it for a change."

"Good afternoon, merfolk." Beresford decided to ignore the commentary. "I am honoured by your reception of me, a mere human." He hesitated but pressed on, despite the absurdity. "I bring a gift of Beresford plum jam."

He held aloft a jar, gleaming red in the sunlight. It was the biggest one on board the *Crescent*, and he only hoped it would do the trick. Just as he knew it would, lasciviousness sharpened the eyes of the female watchers as he lifted the jar.

"So generous and noble," said one.

"So kind and strong," said another.

Another licked her lips. "Mmm, Beresford Jam," she said. "Even in our corner of the sea, we have heard of it."

"Yes, because I told you about it," said Seraphine tartly. "Now, Mistress Viola, please tell us what you have heard about my brother."

Mistress Viola – the teal-haired leader – slipped off her rock and swam quickly over to Beresford. He backed away, but she only snatched the jam out of his hand. Retreating to her rock, she hugged her new treasure close to her breast and smiled. "Your brother, the High Prince? Why, nothing, of course. What should we hear about your brother?"

Seraphine glared. "You implied you knew something!"

"I know his highness is always seeking out mischief," said Mistress Viola. "No doubt Jaq is in some trouble of his own making."

This was Beresford's own thought, but Seraphine was outraged. "How dare you say that! We received a ransom note."

"Maybe he wrote it himself," shrugged another mermaid. This one had very light colouring: her hair was so pale green it was almost blonde in the sun. Beresford turned his eyes resolutely away from the long, lithe form so sparingly clad. The mermaid blinked her pale eyes at him and languidly waved a hand-mirror in a seductive movement.

"Ethel!" said Seraphine. "Behave yourself and take that insulting remark back! My brother would not write his own ransom note! And tell us what you *do* know."

The pale-haired mermaid named Ethel shook her head at Seraphine and said nothing.

Mistress Viola shrugged. "First, some refreshments. We do not forget our manners, even if you do, *Your Highness*. Please sit, and we will drink to your mother's health and try this famous jam. Then we can talk."

Seraphine sat petulantly, clutching her red towel around her and tossing her black curls. Beresford took a spot with his back to the sun so he could watch them all without impediment. He didn't want to be surprised by any untoward movements. A younger mermaid proceeded to pour a sparkling liquid into clamshells. These were passed around, nursed carefully by all who received one.

"Mermaid tears?" asked Seraphine, holding her clam in two hands. Beresford copied her so as not to breach etiquette inadvertently.

"Only a tear each," said Madame Viola. "The rest is green tea. You need not worry that you will become wailed."

Beresford looked enquiringly at Seraphine. She shrugged. "It is a type of Heightener. A stimulant, if you will. It heightens the taste. You needn't worry too much unless it is mixed with another stimulant as well."

He examined the clam suspiciously. The pale liquid glimmered. "You will excuse me if I refuse to partake of a magical drink from mermaids."

Ethel giggled. "Oh, it won't harm you, my lord. Do not turn down our hospitality, I beg you."

Seraphine sighed. "It is fairly harmless. You will still be yourself, with your wits about you. Do not be afraid."

Beresford did not want to be called a coward, nor did he want to be teased into foolishness. After considering the matter carefully – and remembering the star in his pocket – he nodded. Seraphine would not lie to him; she had promised him that, and she needed his help. "Very well."

The mermaids all smiled approvingly. Ethel of the

pale-green hair fluttered her eyelids slowly. It looked odd, as if she were mimicking a gesture that was unnatural to her. With a start, Beresford realised that she did not have eyelashes: mermaids probably did not need them as humans did, being underwater creatures.

Mistress Viola held her clam up. "To Queen Glowdon. And good birthday wishes to the High Princess Seraphine."

Everyone raised their cups and drank, including Beresford.

The tea was fragrant, with a light, clear flavour. Unusual, but refreshing. No drowsiness or confusion immediately resulted, but he waited a while before taking another sip.

The mermaids watched avidly as Mistress Viola doled out small scoops of jam onto what appeared to be seaweed biscuits. Beresford claimed to be content with his tea, but Seraphine munched happily on her piece. Various feminine tones murmured expressions of delight at the flavour of the jam. Beresford shifted uncomfortably under the appreciative glances coming his way. Damn jam. It always garnered too much attention.

Fortunately, one of the mermaids changed the subject, laughing at Seraphine. "We saw your brother on your birthday," she chuckled. "A sight to behold!"

"I do not want to talk about my birthday," said

Seraphine snappishly. "I wish to know where the rascal is now."

Mistress Viola took a long gulp of tea and sighed in satisfaction. "Your Highness, my dear Seraphine, I do not see why we should tell you anything. You must be here without your mother's permission. In fact, I suspect your mother does not know where you are at all. I am almost tempted to take someone hostage myself." Viola's opaque black eyes crinkled with amusement.

The sight was somewhat unnerving, and Beresford shifted on his rock, the wet cloth sticking to his skin. When Ethel cast him a glance, he took another sip of tea.

Seraphine straightened and proceeded to show her royal backbone. "Mistress Viola, you would not want to threaten the Mer-Selkie treaties. I point out that you depend upon our trade. My mother will not hesitate to cut you out if you harm me." Seraphine cast a contemptuous glance at the pile of seaweed and shells on the rock, which Beresford felt was less than tactful. "We can easily learn how to weave our own baskets."

"Such lovely shells you have," he said quickly, taking another sip of tea. "Do you trade those also?"

Mistress Viola wiggled her shoulders playfully, making her blue skin shimmer. "For you, certainly, my lord earl. Is there one you like best? It can be a gift by which to remember us fondly."

Beresford evaluated the shells and became aware that his mind had sharpened slightly. It must be the effect of the tears; he could see the colours and light more clearly. However, it was not a distraction. His wits also felt quicker; he only hoped it wasn't a delusion. Carefully, he tested his mind, conjugating *capio* in all its tenses, and recalling the ship's atlas with surprising clarity.

At the same time, he picked out a shell, a glowing white spiral, luminous in the sunshine. He had noticed it matched the one in Mistress Viola's hair.

"Good choice," she purred. "I found that myself."

Ethel, the mermaid with lighter colouring, held up her small hand-mirror encrusted with tiny pearls. She made a show of peering into it. "The earl is not for you, Viola. My mirror tells me he is destined for a fair lady."

Beresford raised his brows, then lowered them again. Such arts were impossible.

Mistress Viola laughed. "A paltry trick, Ethel, when you are the fairest here. I am sure my lord will be very happy with a darker shade." She ran a hand over her own teal locks.

Beresford cleared his throat and changed the subject. "May I point out – if the prince has indeed been taken hostage by your people, it could precipitate a crisis between you and the selkies. I am sure that is not in your best interests, Mistress Viola."

Mistress Viola heaved a sigh. "Cursed selkies, always so territorial. However, I assure you, my lord, I do not know where their precious prince might be."

Ethel spoke up once more, tucking her mirror away. "I do."

All eyes turned to look at her. She glowered. "He is with Costo."

"I knew it!" said Seraphine. "I have seen them together!"

"So have I," said Ethel, folding her arms. "Too often."

Mistress Viola frowned. "You betray your jealousy, Ethel. Simply because Costo likes spending time with Jaq does not mean he has taken Jaq hostage."

Ethel sniffed. "It is the kind of thing Costo would do."

"Ethel!" declaimed another mermaid. "How can you say that about your lover?"

"Costo is not currently my lover," said Ethel. "How can he be when I never see him? He would rather frolic with a useless selkie prince. They are probably somewhere on the French coast, getting drunk on cognac."

"When did you last see Costo?" demanded Seraphine.

"At your party."

"Everyone was at my party," snapped Seraphine. "Did you see Costo with Jaq?"

"I saw him leave with Jaq, after the ceremony," said Ethel. "Costo was supporting your brother, as if he could not walk."

Seraphine's face paled a little.

Beresford's mind, alight with clarity and insight, risked a question. "French coast, did you say? North or south?"

The strange eyes all turned towards him, along with Seraphine's dark, wide gaze.

Ethel gave him a wink. "South, my lord. Do you know it?"

"Only a little." That was not entirely true. He knew some of it very well. There was one treacherous spot, notorious for shipwrecks. He had scouted around the area in case familiarity should be needed. At the time, he had been confused as to why so many ships had perished there.

The rocky outcrops also grew the same white star-shaped flowers as here. It could be a merfolk haunt. A merlure, Seraphine had called it.

"Your Highness," he said, turning to the selkie. "Perhaps we should leave these gentle ladies to their duties."

"Yes," put in Ethel. "Find Costo. I worry about what he might do if he has Jaq."

Seraphine rose quickly, letting the red blanket slip down. "What do you mean? What do you think Costo might do?"

Ethel shrugged. "I couldn't say for certain. But Jaq doesn't realise how much Costo hates the selkies' power over the merfolk."

Seraphine paled again. Beresford jerked his head. "Let us leave now."

"At once," said Seraphine. "Thank you for your hospitality, Mistress Viola. We appreciated the tea and the tears."

Mistress Viola nodded regally. "Good luck with your quest, Your Highness. And thank you for the jam, my lord earl." She patted the large jar with a pleased smile.

Slowly, Beresford and Seraphine walked back over the rocks to where his ship waited in the water.

"Give me my Star back," demanded Seraphine once they were well out of hearing. The red blanket trailed behind her like a royal cloak, and she held out an imperious hand. "You do not need it anymore."

"Certainly." Beresford pulled the star out of his pocket, where it was warming a patch of his shirt. It made him uncomfortable, to have a hold over Seraphine, and he was glad to return it.

She received it back eagerly, sighing with relief once it was nestled in her hair again.

"I take it you have a plan?" she asked.

"A direction, at least," he replied. "I think Ethel gave us a clue – deliberately."

"We will take whatever hint we can," said Seraphine. "The south coast of France, is it?"

Beresford nodded. "We can be thankful it isn't the north, as that is where Napoleon is gathering his main flotilla, and we would have a tricky time of it. Nonetheless, we shall have to be on the watch." Fortunately, he was prepared for this sort of covert quest. Though he had not braved a merman's den before.

He half-turned one last time before they went out of sight. Mistress Ethel was still watching them, her black eyes now unblinking, her hands still in her lap.

Jaq

Jaq dreamed of the merfolk's song. Its exquisite melody lifted and spun around him with an indefinable, irresistible call. He tossed uneasily, knowing the danger, not wishing to see another human die. His dream conjured a ship, spiralling down to the depths amid the long, flashing tails of the mermen. Costo's face loomed, grinning maliciously, and a tiny, struggling human figure fought against the deep.

Jaq woke with a start. It was not entirely a dream. The sweet, tempting call of the mersong wafted through the cave. He sat up. It had been five days now; it would be too much to expect the Wastrels would not go hunting. Still, he did not want to see what they brought back.

A sound of splashing introduced a dissonance into the song.

Then a voice, all too familiar, echoed in the cave.

"There is no need for all these theatrics," shouted Seraphine. "Can you not see he is coming willingly? Stop it at once!"

Jaq leapt to his feet, his ankles pulling at the rope. "Seraphine? Is that you?"

"Jaq!" Her voice quivered, then strengthened. "You cursed clam-face! Where are you?"

"I'm here," he called helplessly, from the inner cave. "Follow the passage through."

A few long minutes later, a brown seal's head surfaced before Jaq. She stared accusingly, then transformed and stalked up the wet slab. He had never been so glad to see his sister's short, curvy form, even if her fists were clenched in anger.

"What in Hades are you doing here?" Seraphine yelled.

"See for yourself." Jaq gestured to the rope. "Did you miss me, dear sister?"

"Mother is furious! The whole guard is searching for you!"

Costo and Fenner appeared behind Seraphine. "Yet the little lady found us."

She spun towards them. "Did you hurt the human?"

"He is safe for now," said Costo soothingly. "If a bit bedraggled."

Jaq interrupted. "What human?"

"The one who found you," replied Seraphine. "It was only due to his wits that we made it here. It was cursed bad luck that we were caught."

Fenner grinned. "Our little crab sentinels let us know someone was sneaking over the cliffs. We are cleverer than mere Frenchmen, you see."

A deep, irate voice could be heard, projected loudly through the cave. "Seraphine? Where have you gone? Where is she, man? Keep off me, for God's sake!"

Costo called back. "Orrow, let him be. He cannot escape."

"Bring him here," demanded Seraphine.

Fenner grinned. "Yours, is he?"

She shrugged. "Not really."

Costo called back, his voice echoing strangely in the cavern. "Bring him in, Orrow."

After some sounds of altercation and discussion, the human man agreed to be towed through the tunnel to Seraphine and Jaq. He emerged spluttering and scowling, still wearing his land boots. His broad shoulders strained against his soaked white shirt, and his brown hair was plastered to his head.

Lurching onto the dry rock, he stood to his full height and surveyed the company. His grey eyes rested on Jaq, taking in the prince's fine (if Jaq did say so himself) naked form without a blink. Jaq was impressed. Seraphine must have trained him up. Though the English always were unflappable.

"Your Highness, High Prince of Skerry?" The human bowed. "I am the Earl of Beresford. How do you do?"

Jaq raised his brows. "How do you do, my lord? So glad you could join us."

Fenner chuckled, but Costo held up a hand. "An earl, no less? We are honoured. I suppose you are here to rescue his highness?"

Seraphine began speaking furiously, but Beresford spoke louder. "We are here to negotiate for his freedom."

Costo laughed, long and amused. "There is a little morsel of information you have overlooked. Jaq took himself hostage."

There was silence. Seraphine and Beresford turned to look at Jaq.

Jaq folded his arms and glared at Costo, gritting his teeth together.

The merman continued. "His royal highness was in on the game. Jaq doesn't want to be rescued. Half the ransom price goes to him – I suppose he can share that with you if you keep your silence. A thousand guineas will go a long way, even among three. And Jaq might still be able to pay back his debts to us."

Seraphine's eyes were wide. "I do not believe it. My brother is tied up."

"Yes, for verisimilitude's sake," said Costo, grinning. "In case the cavalry arrived. We didn't want the Queen's men to realise Jaq's complicity. But you aren't cavalry, are you? You are extra bargaining chips."

Seraphine turned on her brother. "You pathetic little slug! Did you really do this?"

Jaq shrugged. "I needed the money. And I owed these fellows a bit." More than a bit, especially after that unfortunate dolphin race, but he wasn't going to lay out unnecessary details.

That really did it. For the next ten minutes, Seraphine raged and shouted at him, her face incandescent with fury. Jaq bore it well for a few of those minutes, but soon he was shouting back. The cave echoed and boomed with their voices.

Costo and Fenner watched, grinning. Beresford stood stock still, his face impassive.

Finally, Seraphine recalled her audience and ground to a halt in her expletives and indictments. She turned her fire on Costo. "Jaq never would have done it if it weren't for you!"

Costo smiled. "I have always been a good influence on your brother."

Beresford spoke at last. "Is this really true? Your Highness?"

"Please, call me Jaq." He winked at Beresford, allowing his gaze to travel over the tall figure. The man didn't blush or move. The earl was going to turn to stone if he wasn't careful. Jaq sighed. "I am afraid it is true. A lark, conceived in a somewhat ... inebriated ... state of mind. I am sorry you have been dragged into my foolery."

"Your *foolery* ..." Seraphine began again, but Beresford interrupted, holding up a hand before she could launch into full attack.

"You do not wish to escape?" Beresford asked.

The whole venture had gone too far, Jaq admitted to himself, and he was privately concerned about Costo's true motives. A rescue would be quite opportune, though he wasn't going to say as much to Seraphine. Jaq shrugged, indicating his tied ankles. "Whether or not I wish to leave, I find myself constrained to this rock."

"And you, my lord and lady, likewise find yourself constrained," said Costo. "Two royals are better than one, I always say. And a human lord might be delicious." His fisheyes rotated towards the earl.

Jaq saw Beresford blink. At last. Jaq took pity on him. "Costo does not really eat humans," he said. "However, I am bound to warn you that not many live to tell of the merfolk. They like to be kept a ... deathly secret."

Fenner chuckled. The sound was eerie in the cave.

Beresford blinked again. Jaq saw him take a deep breath.

"Well then," said the earl. "I suppose we are stuck here for now. Does anyone have any tea?"

No tea was forthcoming. Costo took objection to Beresford's aloof air and insisted the earl and Seraphine be restrained. Threatening to harm Seraphine was enough to gain Beresford's co-operation, though she told him to flee. Both Jaq and Beresford had to watch as Seraphine, shrieking, was overcome by Orrow and Fenner and tied to the same rock in the inner cave. This time, their wrists, as well as their ankles, were bound.

Jaq watched proceedings, sick to his stomach. He tried to talk reason to Costo, telling him matters had gone too far. But the merman was intractable. "I want those guineas," he said. "And failing that, I want to cause a ruckus no one will forget. Two royals make wonderful gambling chips, to my mind. Who knows what I could achieve?"

Jaq swallowed, aware that Seraphine was watching with fire in her eyes.

The mermen secured their bonds, then left the three alone in the cave, with only the glow-worms to light their faces.

"What do you think Costo meant by that last comment?" hissed Seraphine.

Jaq chewed on his lower lip. "Possibly he wants to negotiate changes to the treaties," he suggested carefully.

The earl spoke up, sandwiched between two naked royals. "It won't come to that," he said. "And at least I have my clothes on. I only wish the same could be said of you two. Your Majesties," he added, in a somewhat ironic tone.

"I am comfortable enough," said Jaq nonchalantly. "Selkies don't feel the cold."

Beresford would be feeling it, Jaq knew. Humans were so frail. But the earl did not complain or shiver. Yet.

Seraphine was still angry. "I can't believe you played such a trick, Jaq. You put us in this position! The whole kingdom is sick with worry, and you were just playing a prank! And now Costo has both of us."

Jaq pressed his lips together. He didn't want to believe that Costo would harm either of them. Yet he had seen a glint in the merman's eye that was unsettling: too cold, even for a fisheye.

Beresford spoke calmly. "It is concerning. Let us turn our minds to how to escape."

"I like your optimism," said Seraphine gloomily. "We are stuck. Even if we untie these ropes, those cursed mermen will be guarding the outer cave."

Jaq heaved a sigh. "I am sure Mother will find us before it turns nasty. You were stupid to bring a human into it, Seraphine. You and I can last here a lot longer than him."

"Don't call *me* stupid!" snapped Seraphine. "Anyway, we can't even take seal form with these ropes around us. We will suffer as well, stuck in human shape."

It was true, though not as much as Lord Beresford. Better not to dwell on it. "How did you find me?" asked Jaq.

"We went to the merlagoon," replied Beresford. "One of the mermaids said you would be with Costo."

"Which mermaid was that?"

"Ethel. The pale, green-haired one," said Seraphine. "Green with envy, I might add. She doesn't like you having Costo's attention. And she implied Costo had some dastardly game afoot. She was kind enough to direct us towards the south French coast. Lord Beresford did the rest."

The earl grumbled. "Succeeded in getting us caught, you mean. I was so concerned with the frogs I didn't think to worry about the crabs."

But Jaq was impressed. "You knew this place?" Even he didn't know this place. "We are on the south French coast?"

Beresford nodded. "Near a notorious shipwreck cove."

"Ah."

"How is it you didn't know?" asked Beresford. "I thought you came willingly."

Jaq shrugged. "I made the plan with them. When it came to execution, I am afraid I was rather ... incapacitated. They brought me here while I was asleep."

"Ha," said Seraphine. "Completely unconscious, you mean."

Jaq changed the subject. "Where is your ship, my lord?"

Beresford shifted on the rock. "We left it hidden in a cove a few miles south and came by foot. I hope these Wastrels don't go after my ship or my men."

There was a silence.

"Is there much of value on your ship?" asked Jaq.

"Only jam," said the earl. "And some bottles of cognac."

"Oh, the Beresford plum jam?" Jaq winced. "Better not let the mermen find out about *that*."

Beresford sighed. "I can see I am going to come out of this adventure with decimated supplies."

Later, the earl fell asleep. Jaq could see he resisted, but Beresford was worn out and eventually succumbed. His deep chest rose evenly, and his head lolled back on the cold rock.

Jaq lowered his voice to whisper over the slumbering form, glaring at Seraphine. "How in Amphitrite's seas did you persuade him to join you?"

Seraphine raised her brows. "How do you think? I took my clothes off." Jaq rolled his eyes, and she giggled. "Lord Beresford only agreed so I would put them back on. His lordship is a complete prude – just like Nannine said humans would be. He does not appear to be much taken by my charms."

"You are impossible," Jaq hissed. "You should not have brought him into it!"

"What else was I supposed to do? You disappeared!"

"Forget about me! I had it all in hand."

"How was I to know that you were complicit in it, you stupid eel?" Seraphine drew a deep breath, and her tone changed. "And the last time we spoke ... I ... said some terrible things. I had to find you, in case you thought I meant them."

Jaq tipped his head, touched. "I know you didn't mean them." He paused. "I didn't mean to embarrass you on your birthday either. I'm sorry, Seraph."

The childhood name seemed to make her more uncomfortable. She frowned. "There's something I haven't told you."

Jaq looked a question, but she was reluctant to continue. "What, Seraphine? Is Mother ill? Raphael?"

"No, no." She bit her lip. "On the day of my birthday, someone gave me a bottle of tears."

"Oh?" Even as Jaq said it, an inkling of what she was about to say came to him. He sat up straight.

"I ... put some in your skerrysun."

His eyes widened. "*You* did?"

Seraphine nodded.

"You ...!" Words failed him. "How much?"

"I don't know! I just tipped a bit in. Maybe a tablespoon."

Jaq banged his head on the rock behind him. "Oh Lamia. I can't believe it! No wonder I was completely wailed beyond a spout! You deserved that mess I made of your birthday." He snapped his gaze back onto her. "Did you know what would happen?"

She spoke in a small voice. "A little."

"You *knew*? You knew it would turn me into a complete fool?"

Seraphine nodded, avoiding his gaze.

"Why?"

"I wanted you to take a backstep for once." Finally, she met his eyes. "You are always such a favourite. Mother's favourite. Everyone's favourite. I didn't want you to outshine me on my own birthday."

"Seraphine, that's ridiculous," Jaq shouted, forgetting the sleeping Beresford. "I couldn't outshine you on your own Age Day!"

"Well, you did," she said bitterly. "Just in a different way."

"You have your own self to blame. Serves you right – you were trying to humiliate me, and the clownfish came home to the coral!"

"Yes, but you took yourself hostage! That *really* stole the show. You're infuriating. Do you think anyone speaks of my Age Day party now?" Seraphine glared at him again. "My only hope is that it will ensure Mother doesn't make you the heir."

"Mother isn't going to make me the heir," said Jaq. "You're the *girl*. We've always had Queens."

"Mother is a radical. And she adores you. Though after this, she might have second thoughts."

"Well, I don't want to rule. I'd rather race with the mermen."

Seraphine growled. "Do you ever think of anyone except yourself?"

Jaq shut his eyes, too tired and angry to face her anymore.

Between them, Beresford cleared his throat. He must have woken with their arguing. "A good birthday party, was it?" he enquired.

CHAPTER 9

Beresford

Beresford was cold. His clothes were still wet. There was not much chance of them drying in this damp cave. A chill draft made matters worse, cutting right to his bones. He might be better off without clothes, like his companions.

He examined Jaq, whose eyes were now closed. Beresford ought to have expected the royal prince to be completely naked. Unlike his sister, the selkie was slender and muscled, but he had the same dark hair, high cheekbones, and striking eyes. A pretty boy. His mother would be beside herself. Especially now that Beresford had managed to get the princess captured as well.

Still, there must be some way out. The fact that he could feel a cool draft probably meant there was another way through, on the land side.

Beresford voiced this thought to the others. They blinked at him blearily.

Jaq was unenthusiastic. "It is probably a tiny cranny, big enough only for an eel."

"That means you can escape, Jaq," said Seraphine nastily.

Beresford gave her a reproving look. "We need a plan. I assume we do all want to escape? Your Highness?"

"Call me Jaq," insisted the prince, "given that you have put yourself out on my behalf. I admit I am currently not enjoying myself. Yet I do not see how we will escape. These ropes aren't much, but the entrance is guarded."

Water was lapping at Beresford's feet, and it now covered some of the rock. "May I enquire how far the tide will rise?"

Jaq grimaced. "Only a few metres. It leaves enough space to breathe. You won't drown. Just get very cold and wet."

Beresford decided he wasn't looking forward to that. "We must find where the draft originates." He began inching the small knife out of the sole of his boot, though it was difficult with his hands tied behind his back. "Tell me what you know about these mermen. How many are here?"

"There are seven Wastrels," said Jaq. "I imagine two of them are posted on the outer entrance and two are guarding the inner passageway."

"Unless they are all gambling," pointed out Seraphine.

"Hm," said Beresford. "Also, they do not have legs, like us. If there is a way through to the rocks, they might not know about it."

"That's true," said Seraphine, impressed. "We have legs." She wriggled hers, and Beresford carefully kept his gaze down, concentrating on obtaining the knife from his boot.

"Costo is the leader," said Jaq. "The others follow his decree. They might have doubts about the whole venture, too, especially if Costo is trying to overturn the Mer-Selkie treaties. If we overcome Costo, we might have a chance."

"We are unlikely to find him alone," replied Beresford, cutting a finger but managing to slip the blade out. He started sawing at the ropes around his feet.

"Costo is dangerous," Seraphine said with a shiver. "All merfolk look cold, but he *is* cold."

Beresford glanced at Jaq to see if he agreed with this judgment. Reluctantly, the boy nodded. "Costo is ruthless. He once had a whole ship's crew killed, rather than waste Lethe charms on them."

"Lethe charms?"

"To make them forget," said Seraphine. "That was a human crew. Costo would hesitate to actually kill *us*. It would warrant his death."

Or cause a war, thought Beresford, but he didn't voice that particular thought.

Jaq might have had the same thought, but instead, he snapped at his sister. "Costo might not kill *us*, but in case you hadn't noticed, Lord Beresford is human. Costo will use that against us. It will be very difficult to leave this cave with his lordship alive. Which is *your* fault, Seraphine."

Beresford kept working at the rope. "So I am our weakest link."

"Of course."

He let out a chuckle under his breath. "We'll see."

The prince raised his eyebrows. "Oh, really?"

"I have unsuspected gifts," said Beresford.

"Such as?"

He grinned. "Plum jam."

Seraphine giggled, slightly hysterically, then sobered. "You want to offer jam in order to escape? We are talking about two thousand guineas here! Possibly five thousand, now they have *me*. They won't exchange that for some jam!"

"The Beresford Jam is highly sought after."

"You're mad," said Jaq.

The rope frayed at last. Beresford slipped his ankle

out and rolled it in the air. "Look, I'm making progress. More than can be said of you two."

Jaq stared. "How did you do that?" he demanded.

"A useful little knife from the sole of my boot," said Beresford, and he began on the trickier task of the ropes around his wrists.

Seraphine began struggling with her own ropes. "You're mad, but I like your spirit."

"Likewise, Your Highness," said Beresford. "I'll cut your hands free as soon as I am able."

Jaq grumbled and watched with reluctant admiration. "Here, pass me the knife. I'll help."

Between the two of them, they had almost cut all the knots before the mermen returned.

There was hardly any warning. Merfolk could certainly sneak up on one. Costo's blue head emerged right near Beresford, making him jump.

The merman flicked blue hair out of his face. "A bit nervous, your lordship? Trying to escape, are you?"

"Just stretching our legs." Beresford suited action to words, sitting down to hide the gleam of the small blade and stretched his feet out before him. Better not to appear as a threat. Unfortunately, this meant sitting in five inches of water. It was icy, and he shuddered.

"There's no way out," said Fenner, behind Costo.

"You're stuck on this little rock here. But how did you sever the ropes?"

"Search them," ordered Costo, and he grabbed Seraphine.

Beresford might have risked a confrontation right there, except Costo also held a long knife. It was a sight longer than his own tiny blade, and it was held to Seraphine's throat. Her large black eyes widened as she winced.

Beresford held up his hands, sighing as Fenner searched him and found the small weapon. Fenner examined it. "This appears to be the culprit. But no others are hidden that I can see."

Damn it. Next time Beresford would have to hide a blade in each boot.

Costo released Seraphine, who tumbled back onto the rock. Beresford realised he was becoming quite accustomed to the sight of her naked form; he was too concerned if she had been hurt to be properly scandalised. She gave him a shaky smile.

Costo snorted. "Ah, my lord, you are a canny one. But you will find you cannot go far from here. The exit is well guarded." He turned dismissively. "Now, Jaq, we need some of your hair."

Jaq raised his brows. "Excuse me?"

"Your lovely black hair. Your mother wants proof that we actually have you in our possession."

Two pairs of dark, regal eyes stared at the merman.

Beresford repressed a smile at the identical looks of complete disdain.

Jaq spoke at last. "I do not think so."

Fenner held up a knife, grinning. "It won't hurt, Your Highness. Just be glad we are not taking your Star."

"You would not dare." Jaq folded his arms, and there was an icy glint in his eye. "You know I would rather die."

Fenner shrugged in acknowledgment. Beresford guessed such an act was far too taboo, even for these blackguards.

"Nevertheless, this is my *hair* we are talking about," said Jaq. He tilted his head, and the long, thick locks fell across his face. Even Beresford had to admit it was luscious. Though he preferred blondes, of course. And females.

"You cannot cut his hair," agreed Seraphine. "Very bad form."

"My pride and joy," said Jaq, making a show of stroking his hair and tossing it back over his shoulder. Beresford caught a glimpse of something shining: a star, hidden underneath.

"Don't be so vain," said Costo. However, Fenner looked a little reluctant to touch the glorious royal locks. Costo frowned and brandished his own knife. "If you won't do it, I'll do it for you."

Costo leaned out of the water, close to Jaq. The

prince scuttled backward to the other end of the tiny rock. "Oh no, you don't."

Costo sighed, and fast as lightning, manoeuvred to reach Jaq. Jaq was faster. Beresford raised a brow. The good-for-nothing prince had quick reflexes.

"Fenner," growled Costo. "Catch him."

Reluctantly, Fenner moved around to trap Jaq. Beresford, sitting in the middle, made his tone amused. "Is this a game of catch the seal?"

Jaq shot him a look and, in one swift motion, dived into the water. Even as Costo lunged towards him, Jaq turned into a seal. It was impressive. Beresford only wished he could do the same. Then he might have a chance of swimming out of here. Perhaps it *was* true that he was a liability.

Costo snarled. "Fine. If you won't give me hair, I'll take some flesh. See what your queen says about *that*." He waved the knife and narrowed his eyes at the seal at the other end of the cave. "Fenner, catch him. We'll take a bit of his tail instead."

"No!" shouted Seraphine. "Don't hurt him! Have some of my hair instead."

In the water, Jaq darted out of Fenner's grasp. The sea churned as they chased each other around the cave. Beresford was almost concerned that one of them would smack their heads onto the walls, but neither did.

Costo turned to Seraphine and growled. "Your hair will do just as well. Hold it out, my pretty princess."

He swam over. Beresford debated leaping to Seraphine's defence, but he reluctantly decided against it. His leg was cramping from the cold, for one thing, and Seraphine had more than enough hair, whereas he only had one chance to fool these mermen.

With a gulp, Seraphine held out a lock between trembling fingers. In a quick gesture, Costo severed it, holding up the curling black prize.

"Fenner! We have what we need."

Jaq, finding himself no longer pursued, stuck his head out of the water. His seal face took on a dumbfounded expression as his gaze landed on Seraphine and Costo.

The merman smirked. "Thank you, Your Highness."

Jaq became human in a swirl of water. "What did you do? How dare you!"

"Your sister offered," said Costo. "So kind. We will be off now. I have a little parcel to send to your mother. Just be glad it doesn't contain part of your hide."

With an insolent splash of their tails, the mermen disappeared. The two royals, enraged, stared after them.

Beresford tried to cheer them up. "Pity they

wouldn't take my hair. Not princely enough, I suppose."

Jaq turned on Beresford, his black eyes snapping. "Why did you not defend my sister?"

"It went against the grain," Beresford admitted. "I was thinking of the long game. There is no point in becoming incapacitated over a lock of hair. Now they have left us alone again."

Seraphine slipped into the water with a petulant sigh. "His lordship is right. I am going to look around."

She slid under, and shortly afterwards, the form of a seal could be seen swimming away from the rock.

Jaq frowned. "You shouldn't have brought Seraphine here."

"I thought you said *she* shouldn't have brought *me* here."

Jaq folded his arms. "*Neither* of you should have ...! I was fine until you two turned up!"

"If you say so."

"I'm going into the water."

"Good. My man Polkins has his wedding in four days, and he is stuck on my ship out there. We are running out of time." Again, Beresford didn't mention the likelihood of war: he rather thought Jaq was well aware of the possibility.

Jaq hunched a shoulder and splashed sulkily into the sea. Soon two seals were methodically exploring the cave. Beresford stood up, the water now halfway up his shins. He turned his gaze to the ceiling. He thought he could make out a darker patch near the back corner of the cave, about three yards above sea level.

His eyes were now fully adjusted to the dark. The glow-worms lit the crevices, showing the size of the cave to be about twenty square yards, with the roof another body length above him. That would change soon with the tide, which might enable him to investigate that interesting back corner. No cracks of sunlight showed, but the draft still blew, cold and bitter over his skin.

The sound of the water lapping against the rocks was a constant murmur, and Beresford had to admit it was making him feel uneasy, to know the tide was rising.

Seraphine emerged near his feet as a human. She blinked water out of her eyes. "There are two mermen guarding the other end of the tunnel, in the outer cave. And possibly another two at the entrance. It will be hard to fight our way out."

Jaq popped up next to her. "I can't find any other entrance below."

"Of course you can't," sniffed Seraphine. "We are trapped."

"Let us try the ceiling and walls," suggested Beresford. "The tide will lift us."

"That is another few hours away," objected Jaq. He

sighed. "You're going to freeze to death before then, you paltry human."

Beresford would have liked to argue, but he rather suspected it was true. "Perhaps if I run on the spot?" he suggested, though that didn't seem wise. It would burn up his little remaining energy.

Jaq pursed his lips. "I am afraid we are going to have to become rather intimate, my lord."

Beresford raised his brows. "Excuse me?"

"As seals, of course. We will keep you warm."

Seraphine giggled, embarrassed. "We?"

Jaq turned to look at his sister. "If we are on either side of him, we will keep him alive."

"I am a lady and a princess!" objected Seraphine. "I'm not going to cuddle up to Lord Beresford! Not as a seal anyway."

Beresford spoke coldly. "Certainly not as either."

"Do you want to live?" asked Jaq. "If so, you are going to have to lower your standards. As for you, Seraph, having placed his lordship in mortal danger, the least you can do is to keep him alive."

With that, Jaq shifted into seal form and advanced up the rock. Beresford's eyes widened. Having a large brown seal waddle towards him with intent was slightly unnerving. He swallowed. However, now was not the time for gentlemanly hysterics. The prince was right. If Beresford stayed as he was in the rising tide, he would die of cold.

The seal nosed up to him, his black eyes amused. Beresford backed up against the rock, sat down, and held out an arm.

The seal shuffled into it.

"What a pretty picture," said Seraphine tartly. Then she sighed. "Very well. If I must, but you can *never* talk to anyone of this." She transformed and lurched up the rock.

Soon Beresford was propped between two brown, fat seals. The sensation of their slippery, warm skin was odd but reassuring.

"Don't worry," he said into the hollow, echoing cave. "I won't tell anyone if you don't."

Jaq

Two hours later, they were floating above the rock, still clinging together. Jaq decided the ceiling might now be within reach. He considered transforming into human form where he was, all snuggled up to his lordship, but thought better of it. Best not to test the earl's *sang froid* too far. Jaq slipped out from under Beresford's arm and splashed loudly away.

"Time to investigate the ceiling," he announced, once human.

Beresford, lurching a little now that he was one seal short of a raft, nodded. "I'll take the back corner."

Seraphine transformed as well, without the same

consideration Jaq had shown. Beresford gave a yelp and swallowed a mouthful of water. "My apologies, Your Highness," he said, once he had spluttered it out.

"My fault," said Seraphine airily. "You couldn't help it if your hand was in an improper place. I'll take the left-hand side of the cave."

They stayed human, for fingers were better at searching the crevices. Beresford swam proficiently to the narrowing back of the cave, but Jaq could see the earl was struggling to stay afloat while examining the roof. Jaq resisted the urge to go over and help, and he turned to focus on his own stretch.

Now that the roof was half a yard away, it was easier to see past the luminescence and find the lines and fissures. One was quite deep. Jaq held his face close to it, to see if the breeze would brush his cheek. The gap was too small for any of them, so he was thankful to find that the breeze did not emanate from there.

Seraphine called out that she had found a hole, but it too was too small even for an eel.

From his end of the cave, Beresford sounded thoughtful. "I think there is a passageway at the back, perhaps carved by a stream. It is big enough for you, Jaq. Perhaps even you, Seraphine."

Jaq swam over to inspect. "It might narrow further into the rock."

Seraphine also investigated. "Your shoulders are too broad, my lord."

"It will have to be Jaq," agreed Beresford.

At that moment, Jaq saw the dark shape of a merman in the water below, and he gave a quick warning. It was Fenner who emerged with a plop. The three captives immediately did their best to look like they were enjoying an entirely innocent float around the cave.

"What are you lot up to?" asked Fenner. "You know there is no way out. Jaq, you are wanted in the other cave."

Jaq, lazily splashing around on his back, looked up. "Me? Why? Lusting after my hair again? I warn you; I won't forgive Costo for that insult to my sister."

"You are needed for a game," said Fenner. "We thought you're probably bored in here with the tide rising. Either that or plotting your escape. You're to join us for another game of craken."

Seraphine's black eyes narrowed. "Have you been playing cards with these villains?" she demanded.

Jaq shrugged. "It passed the time."

She glared at him. "Of course it did. I suppose you had mermaid tears along with it."

"No, I had enough of that from you," snapped Jaq.

Beresford was swimming on the spot. Jaq could see his lordship was trying not to shake with the cold. "Can I play too?" asked the earl.

Fenner glanced over sceptically. "You?"

"Yes." Beresford looked down his nose at the merman, which was not easy, considering he was paddling furiously with his inadequate human legs while Fenner swirled his tail gently. Jaq's opinion of the earl went up another notch. "I am good at cards."

"You don't know craken," said Fenner.

"I can learn."

"Go on," said Jaq. "It might make things interesting. Unless you are scared that the earl will beat you at your own game?"

Fenner grinned. "You'll have to teach his lordship, Jaq. And if he's no good, he has to come back here."

"What about me?" shrieked Seraphine. "You're going to leave me here alone?"

"Girls don't play craken," said Fenner. "You stay here. You are insurance for these two behaving themselves next door."

Seraphine started ranting. Jaq hoped she wouldn't overdo it and rouse Fenner's suspicion. Apparently, however, Fenner assumed Seraphine was the type to have a royal tantrum and ignored her.

"I will check with Costo," he said and disappeared with a flick of his long tail.

The three waited, Seraphine still half-heartedly objecting, in case Fenner should be listening as he swam away. After a minute, she stopped.

"You will keep them busy?" she asked, her eyes

alight with a look Jaq knew well. "I'll try the passageway."

"I don't like it," said Beresford. "But it is the best we have. Here, take my shirt."

Seraphine's brow wrinkled in confusion. "Why?"

"If you emerge in France, you will need something to wear. And if you run into trouble, you can show any difficult Frenchmen the fleur-de-lis pin in the pocket. It should grant you safety for a short while."

Jaq raised his brows at this evidence of further hidden depths to the earl. Beresford avoided his gaze, so Jaq forbore to question him further on his alliances. The main concern now was the Wastrels, not the French.

Seraphine also quirked her eyebrow. "Well, my lord, if it means you finally take your clothes off like the rest of us ..."

Beresford frowned at her and stripped off his white shirt. She accepted the sodden mass, grinning. "Admirable form."

Beresford spoke repressively. "You should know that I prefer blondes."

"Oh really?" said Jaq with interest. "Me too."

Seraphine huffed and put on the shirt. She fingered the pin inside the pocket to assure herself it was there.

Beresford turned to Jaq. "Do you think you and I can overpower seven mermen?"

"Unlikely," said Jaq. "Merfolk are strong. So are

selkies. You won't be a match for them, even if you still had that little knife."

"It will have to be our wits," said Beresford contemplatively. "And I have an idea if you will countenance it."

Jaq bent his head closer and listened to Beresford's plan. Reluctantly, he agreed. Too soon, they were interrupted by Fenner's head surfacing near the passage entrance.

The merman raised his voice. "Costo wants to know if you have anything to gamble."

Beresford turned. "Yes, indeed."

"What?"

"Plum jam."

To be safe, Jaq turned into a seal so he could drag the earl through the passageway quickly after Fenner. It wasn't a very long distance, but the human was cold and weak, and he had already been swimming for a while.

Beresford took the seal tail proffered to him with good grace, which Jaq was pleased to see. There was no point in wasting vital energy on pride – unless it was regarding one's hair, of course.

When they emerged in the front cave, Jaq saw it had a much higher ceiling, made of white rock that reflected the waves' glimmer. Five Wastrels leaned their elbows on a rock in the centre, with water lapping up to their ribs: Costo, Fenner, the dark green Orrow, and two more who Jaq recognised as Ivel and Luth by their shades of blue. Two more mermen must yet guard the entrance.

Light crept in from the mouth of the cave, a tantalising shimmer hinting at freedom.

Costo tossed the craken bones as five sets of fisheyes turned to examine Jaq and Beresford as the two approached. For a moment Jaq realised how alien and unnerving the sight must be to the earl: five mermen with blue or green skin, their hair lank down their backs like seaweed, and their tails long and powerful in the water. Meanwhile Lord Beresford clung like a seal-pup to Jaq's tail.

Jaq became human and decided to take the offensive.

"Have you any food?" he demanded. "We are starving. If you want a good game, you had better give us something to eat." Beside him, Beresford nodded.

Costo tutted. "Always expecting royal treatment, Your Highness. I thought *you* were providing the food. What's this I hear about jam?"

"The Beresford Plum Jam," said the earl. Jaq was fairly certain Beresford spoke in capitals. So the earl couldn't be *too* unnerved by his circumstances.

Fenner nodded. "I've heard of it. Pretty ripe stuff, from all accounts."

"Of course, you have heard of it," Jaq said.

Beresford cleared his throat modestly. "The most highly sought-after English jam in history." Jaq rather thought his lordship was playing up the pomposity too much, but he nodded solemnly in agreement.

"How much do you have?" asked Costo.

"Twenty jars."

One of the mermen let out a low whistle.

"Why?" asked Costo. "I mean, why do you have so much? And where is it?"

"I was going to trade it with the French for cognac. It is on my ship, not far from here."

"Yes, we know where your ship is," said Costo. He folded his arms on the rock. "We could simply take it."

"You'd rather play for it," said Jaq. "Like a true Wastrel. What's the fun in luring an innocent crew when you could play craken for the prize instead?"

Costo laughed. "Very well. We will play for both the ship and the jam. And anything else on the vessel. You have five minutes to give his lordship the basics, Jaq." He tossed Jaq the bones.

"Food first," said Jaq. "And for Triton's sake, something to drink."

CHAPTER 11

Beresford

Twenty minutes later, Beresford had eaten his fill of fermented seaweed, dried seaweed chips, and stewed squid. He didn't care for the flavours, but he could feel the sustenance warming his body slightly. And it was a relief to be sitting on a stone seat, though he was still half-submerged in water.

Even better, he now held a goblet of whiskey, also warming, while Jaq explained the rules of craken to him.

The game was complex, involving pairing symbols with different values. As Jaq listed the values once more, Beresford raised his voice slightly.

"What of the mermaid tears? I have heard much talk of them lately. Can I sample those too?"

"Certainly," said Orrow. He swam around with a crystal bottle and held it over Beresford's cup of whiskey, tipping in a few drops. "Careful, your lordship." Orrow winked. "The tears make your drink more powerful."

"Ah, good," said Beresford. "I'm in need of a powerful drink."

Just as Beresford thought, the effect of the tears was almost instantaneous. He had a good stomach for whiskey, so a mere goblet of it did not affect him. However, with the tears swirling in the drink, his mind sharpened as it had at the lagoon. Soon he had a good grasp of craken - the rules and the possible strategies - under Jaq's expert tutelage.

The game began. Beresford did his best to act both earnest and increasingly drunk. Jaq, sitting opposite, helped by glancing at Beresford's goblet and looking increasingly worried.

It was easy to lose the first few bottles of jam, then bet more and lose them again while determining the style of the other players. Costo was a bit reckless, which was helpful. Fenner was very deliberate, but perhaps too cautious. Orrow was cheerful and inattentive. The two other blue mermen, Ivel and Luth, were harder to read. They also partook of tears along with Beresford, but he did not know if it would have the same effect on them.

From what Jaq had told him, the tears usually heightened the taste and potency of the drink, not the mind of the drinker. Perhaps it was different for humans, for the earl's mind was balanced and sharp.

Beresford kept a frown on his face, but he let his gaze wander and made foolish remarks.

"I hear the High Princess had a good party the other day?"

"Oh yes," said Fenner. "Much revelry was had by all."

Orrow snickered. "With theatrical entertainment provided by Jaq here."

Jaq frowned at his bones. "I had a bit too much to drink, that's all."

"Coral cutthroat?" asked Luth, staring at his own hand.

Jaq shrugged. "Maybe that. Maybe something else."

Ivel smiled. "Looked like you were on a gallon of skerrysun."

"Skerrysun? What is that?" asked Beresford, though he had a good idea from hearing Jaq and Seraphine talk about it.

"The traditional selkie drink," explained Ivel. "It makes you *very* happy."

"Mayhap it was mixed with tears," said Orrow. "Jaq here was a bit *too* happy."

"Pity his sister wasn't," put in Costo. "Nor his mother, no doubt."

Beresford tilted his head curiously. "Do you have any now? Can I try this skerrysun too?"

"Ooh, his lordship is eager," said Fenner. "We have a flask of sunshine, don't we, Costo?"

"You'll have to win it," said the leader, and he jerked his head for Ivel to fetch it.

The flask was silver, the size of Beresford's arm. Somehow, he managed to win it in the next round, careful to make it seem as if it were almost an accident.

"Beginner's luck!" Ivel handed the silver flask over.

Beresford held it up. "You'll all have some, won't you?" He splashed liberal amounts into their whiskey. Jaq eyed him in speculation, so Beresford gave the selkie a wink. "For you, Your Highness?"

"Not today." Jaq shuddered.

Beresford poured his own generous serve and turned back to his hand of bones. "Er, what does the snake symbol mean again?"

Fenner explained, and the game moved on.

The good thing about playing half-submerged in water was that it was easy to pour one's drink away without calling attention to it. Beresford tipped his skerrysun into the ocean, pretending to drink it in one go. He certainly didn't want to add anything else to the mix currently surging through his blood. A few mermaid tears were enough for him.

At least now, for the others, the tears were muddled with skerrysun. If Jaq's experience at Seraphine's birthday was anything to go by, that should make them all a bit more reckless.

Slowly, Beresford began to win a little. Costo gave him a suspicious look, so Beresford lost the next round. However, on the seventh game, he surged ahead, gathering a large win and recouping ten bottles of jam as well as several sovereigns.

"Shame," Beresford said. "I have so much jam back home. How about I put all twenty bottles on the next game?" He smiled merrily as if befuddled on skerrysun. "What are you going to gamble in return?"

On cue, Jaq spoke up. "How about our freedom?" he suggested. "It only seems a fair match for a whole ship and twenty jars."

Beresford frowned. "I didn't say I bet the ship," he objected.

Costo tipped his head. "Throw in the ship, and we'll match it with your freedom, my lord."

Beresford noted the omission. "Mine? What of his highness?"

Costo stared unblinkingly. "Just yours."

Beresford considered. "Mine for the ship, his for the jam."

Fenner laughed. "How do you like being worth twenty bottles of plum jam, Jaq?"

Jaq glowered, but he didn't say anything.

"Do you take me for a fool?" said Costo. "His pretty highness is worth a lot more than that, no matter how good this jam might be. I'll let you play for your own freedom, my lord, but Jaq stays with us. I have plans for him."

Beresford shrugged and smiled happily. "Very well. Do you mind, Jaq? I have a hankering to hie back to my ship."

Costo rubbed his chin. "We will see if that happens."

Jaq shrugged. "You don't deserve to be in this mess, my lord. Win your freedom, if you may."

Beresford risked a question. "So I have your word, Costo, as a – er – gentlemerman that you will let me go if I win? With all my property, including my ship?"

"Don't insult me by asking," snapped Costo. "If I play, I pay. Do I need your word as a gentleman that your ship will be handed over if *I* win?"

Chastised, Beresford shook his head. "Of course not. My apologies."

Costo grinned and dealt the bones again, whistling. Beresford was glad to see the skerrysun had at least some effect on the surly merman. He carefully did not allow his eyes to shift to the light streaming in at the entrance. It must be past dawn now. He was chilled to the bone, and his crew must be wondering what had befallen him. It was time to make an end to this.

The game settled into silence, and the play became serious. Soon Ivel and Fenner were out, and the game narrowed to Jaq, Beresford, Costo, and Luth.

Jaq bowed out, though Costo shot him a look. "Helping your friend to freedom, my prince? Good of you, when he is eager to leave you behind."

"I feel sorry for his lordship," said Jaq shortly.

Luth threw his hand down in disgust. "I don't think you should feel sorry for him," he observed. "He is going to win."

And so Beresford did. It was easy with his mind so sharp and clear, and Costo now even more reckless under the influence of Skerrysun. Beresford put down his final hand in triumph and looked around benignly.

"Ah, there we go. Sorry about that, fellows. I'm happy to leave some jam with you as a token of my respect. You all played well."

Costo smiled reluctantly, his black eyes opaque. "You're a canny one, my lord. We will take your jam if it pleases you."

Beresford nodded. "Well, I suppose I'll swim off now. May I have an escort, someone to fetch the jam back?"

"Not Jaq, if that's what you're thinking," said Costo sharply.

"Ah, there was something I did not mention," said

Beresford politely. "I have Jaq's seal star. I believe that makes him my property, and I'll be taking him with me."

A deathly silence fell over the cave. The sound of the water lapping against the walls became loud.

"Excuse me?" said Costo slowly.

"His highness gave his star into my safekeeping," explained Beresford. "That means Jaq is my vassal now and belongs to my crew."

Everyone turned to stare at Jaq, with expressions of horror.

"You enslaved yourself to this man?" demanded Fenner. "Are you mad, princeling?"

Jaq shrugged. "If I escape this cave alive, Mother will kill me anyway. This way, she can't touch me."

Costo swept the bones off the table in a violent movement. "You're mad but clever. We cannot bend the rules of the stars, even if you show them no respect – and besides, I think you will find, your lordship, that owning a Selkie Star binds you into service as well. You will have to look after his highness now, a task I do not envy you."

Beresford cast a glance at the prince, who shrugged dismissively. Seraphine hadn't mentioned the obligations the star might create. Beresford would have to give it back as soon as possible. "Ah," he said. "That will be my concern. Nothing to bother your head about."

Costo twisted his lips, and Beresford could see the merman was fighting with himself about whether or not to dishonour his promise to the earl. Then Costo spoke slowly. "However, we are cleverer than you. Unless you have Seraphine's Star also?"

Beresford shook his head mournfully. "I am afraid the princess is still your problem."

Fenner laughed but quickly silenced when he became the recipient of Costo's glare.

Costo spoke with great deliberation. "The queen will be delighted to know her children have swapped places. It might even cause the kind of trouble for which I hoped. Are you really going to leave your younger sister here, Jaq? The heir to the throne?"

"You won't dare ransom Seraphine," said Jaq. "And I'll come back with reinforcements before you can escalate this. It won't work, Costo. It is time to abandon the whole lark."

Beresford was glad to hear that Jaq did not imply that Seraphine's life could be in danger; perhaps if they both acted as if it were impossible, Costo would realise his folly. And perhaps Seraphine had managed to find a way through the rocks.

Costo snarled. "How about you leave now, seal pup, or I'll not answer for the consequences. Luth, go with them. Fetch some of that cursed jam."

Luth nodded and swam off. Quickly, Beresford and

Jaq followed, while the opportunity still hung in the balance.

Yet, as they reached the entrance, a new shape showed in the shimmering light, blocking their way.

"Ah," purred Ethel. She flicked her pale green hair over her shoulder. "My Lord Beresford, I'm so pleased to see you again."

CHAPTER 12

Beresford

*B*eresford reared back slightly at the sight of Ethel blinking her pale eyelids at him, her black fisheyes glinting.

"Madame," he said stiffly. "This is not the time for pleasantries."

Costo spoke from behind them. "Ethel! What are you doing here?" His tone sharpened. "How do you know the earl?"

The mermaid swam forward in sinuous, seductive movements. "I know his lordship *very* well. We are *intimately* acquainted."

Beresford turned, almost at the mouth of the cave. "I only met this mermaid a day ago, I swear it."

Ethel sighed. "Yes, and what a day it was. Do you renounce me so soon, my lord?"

Beresford frowned at her. "I cannot imagine what you are implying," he said, though, in fact, he could.

"What do you mean?" growled Costo. "Have you been intimate with *him*, Ethel?"

She ran her fingers through pale hair that floated like seaweed. "What was a mergirl to do? He seduced me with plum jam and those sky-grey eyes."

Jaq intervened, hovering behind Ethel with one eye on the entrance. "Nonsense. Ethel is jealous, Costo. She is avenging herself for your inattention."

Ethel turned on Jaq, lips thinning. "I am not jealous, Your Highness. Look at you all, gambling and drinking, wasting yourselves. I am glad that I never see you. Can you blame me for turning to a human for comfort?"

Costo dove forward with a snarl. He surfaced by Beresford and pushed his nose into the earl's face. "Did you touch this lady, my lord?"

Before Beresford could answer, Costo grabbed him around the neck.

"No!" Beresford choked out the words. "I'm spoken for." Miss Avely's face was swimming before his eyes. He suddenly realised he didn't want to die in a cave in France, never to see her again.

Ethel cast a hand to her forehead. "How can you

say that?" she murmured brokenly. "You didn't tell me your heart was taken, my lord."

"You rake," snarled Costo. "I'll teach you to betray an innocent merwoman."

Beresford would have laughed, for it was the first time he had been accused of seducing an innocent merwoman. However, he was too busy fighting Costo off.

Enraged, the merman was trying to drown him. It was an unfair fight. As Jaq had warned, the merman was supernaturally strong and at ease in the water. Beresford, cold, tired, and sick of swimming, was quickly overpowered, gaining a wrenching injury to his arm in the process.

However, assistance was provided in the form of a selkie prince. Jaq yanked Costo off, and Beresford rose for a gulp of air. He saw Ethel watching with a pleased smile. Jaq and Costo now wrestled in the water with lethal intent.

The selkie and merman were matched in strength. The water churned and splashed, their grunts echoing loudly in the cave.

Beresford tried to swim for the entrance, but the other mermen dove into the fray. Three soon had him encircled and grasped his arms and a leg, making him grimace in pain.

"What, three of you?" objected Beresford. He saw,

to his dismay, that Jaq was now receiving the worst of the fight. Ivel had surged in to help Costo.

Fenner was apologetic. "There is a little matter of a lady's honour."

"I never touched her," Beresford said, from the undignified position of lying on his back. "Let us fetch the jam and be done with this female's foolery."

Fenner looked tempted; however, Luth was unmoved. "Not until Costo is done with you."

Costo held Jaq's head in the crook of his elbow, with Ivel grasping the selkie's other side. It was an odd sight because Jaq was now a seal, though from the way he lolled, it looked as though he had lost consciousness.

A poor showing by the both of them, thought Beresford bitterly.

Costo shouted at Beresford. "Land scum, I should never have played craken with you. Now I will call in your ship the old way. And I will send this prince to Skerry on a funeral raft."

At that moment, the light of the entrance was shadowed once more.

A voice spoke, clear and regal, with a hint of ice. "My son, you must be careful of the company you keep."

CHAPTER 13

Jaq

Jaq's head whipped up. He had only been pretending to be unconscious, waiting for the right moment to act. Typical of his mother to see right through that. Or perhaps she didn't really care if he was almost dead.

Her Majesty swam into the cave, her flowing silver lace cloak streaming over her otherwise naked body.

"Costo, unhand my son."

The merman wrenched Jaq closer, causing him to wince with pain. Costo spoke between gritted teeth. "I don't think so. Jaq swum into my hands, and I will make good use of him."

"Did you really think you could hide from Us?"

The queen's black eyes snapped, and Ivel fell back a length. Jaq felt Costo quiver involuntarily. The queen continued. "You will pay for this, you floor feeder. Release my son at once!"

Jaq decided it was time to assert some authority, now that the merman was distracted. In one smooth, strong movement, Jaq used his tail to thwack Costo on the back and slip out of his grasp.

Costo heaved for breath, floundering. "I still have Seraphine," he spluttered. "And I won't give her back until I have what I want: money or war."

"No, you don't have the High Princess," countered the queen. "And I'm certainly not going to declare war on your unfortunate species because of the actions of its lowest specimen. Arrest him, men. Costo, you will pay for this under the Mer-Selkie treaties, as is right."

Jaq saw twelve of the royal guard had entered the cave after his mother, now swimming in formation behind her. Some were in seal form and some human. If Beresford wasn't yet accustomed to male nakedness, he was shortly to become so. Two of the selkie men grasped the earl, who let out a yelp of pain. Beresford must have been injured in the fight.

Costo resisted viciously but he was quickly overcome, and the rest of the mermen were captured in short order. The cave did not allow many avenues of escape. Briefly, Jaq wondered where Seraphine was.

"Mother ..." he began.

"Are you harmed?" the queen asked, coming closer. Jaq thought he saw a fleeting expression of concern. He put up his hand and felt blood on his forehead.

"I am fine," he said. "However, I fear that the Earl of Beresford is hurt. He came to rescue me, and he is a mere human. Also – "

Costo interrupted, shouting from where he struggled against the selkies who held him. "Jaq came willingly! He was complicit! Ask him!"

The queen turned a thunderous gaze on her son. "Is this true, Jaq?"

He swallowed. "Er. Not exactly. But – er – true enough."

Jaq waited, quaking. His mother's eyes became black flints. She swam in a slow circle around him. The silver lace trailed, a ridiculous waving softness in contrast to the hard voice that now rung out through the cave.

"My son, this goes too far. You must be punished."

Jaq nodded. "Yes, Mother. I agree. However, can we decide on the matter of my punishment later? The human needs assistance."

The queen turned in a swirl to look at Beresford, who hung limply between two selkies.

"What is a human doing here?"

Jaq cleared his throat, not wanting to implicate Seraphine, despite everything. "His lordship came to rescue me. He was caught, but he fought nobly to release me." Jaq decided it was inadvisable to mention the gambling or the tears.

The queen swam in slow strokes over to Beresford. The earl's eyes were wide, his lips blue, and he couldn't stop his icy limbs from shaking. However, he spoke with calm dignity. "Your Majesty. How do you do? A fortuitous meeting."

The queen smiled, amused. "English, are you? Did you try to rescue my useless son?"

"Not entirely useless," said Beresford, teeth chattering. "Jaq was assisting in the escape."

Jaq wondered why he was defending him.

The queen spoke dryly. "Realised he was not worth two thousand guineas?"

"Perhaps."

She swam closer, frowned at Beresford's shivering, and snapped out an order. "Someone wrap the earl in sealskins please, before he faints from the cold."

Beresford looked both affronted and grateful as two of her men hurried to obey. Once he was neatly ensconced in a thick hide and placed on a rock, the queen deigned to continue the conversation. "How did you know my son was in danger?"

Beresford hesitated, shooting a glance at Jaq, who shook his head slightly.

"Someone informed me." Beresford hunched the sealskin closer over his shoulders with a suspicious look, as if it might turn him into a seal. Of course, only seal-stars were capable of that.

"Oh? A selkie?" asked the queen, with an air of curiosity.

"Perhaps."

"Which selkie?"

"I do not really know," said Beresford uneasily.

"My lord, if there is one thing we need to establish, it is that you must not lie to Me."

Beresford gulped. "No, Your Majesty."

"Who told you?"

"Your Majesty, it was in confidence."

She turned away, looking pleased. "It was my daughter. You cannot hide things from Me. Seraphine is being escorted back to Skerry as we speak, scratched and bedraggled from her passage through the rocks and her efforts at evading French discovery."

"Is she hurt?" demanded Jaq.

"Just a few scrapes and bruises, no more than she deserves."

Jaq sighed with relief. "She told you of our whereabouts?"

"Yes, we saw her waving a shirt – yours, I presume, my lord? – from the shore. She was rather pleased to see us. I, on the other hand, was not pleased to see her so far from home."

"I ..."

"Jaq, you have enmeshed both your sister and this

human lord in trouble." The queen held up a hand. "I know Seraphine is also at fault. However, if you had not begun this stupid *prank*, she would not have been compelled to attempt a rescue. Not to mention your ludicrous behaviour on her birthday."

Jaq squirmed. He badly wanted to tell his mother that Seraphine was also partly to blame for that, but he knew there was not much point defending himself. He was in trouble regardless; he might as well let all blame heap upon his head. The only question was how he would be punished.

This was answered almost immediately.

His mother turned to look at Beresford. "Did I hear that you have my son's Selkie Star?"

Beresford glanced at Jaq but could not deny it. "Yes."

"I have decided that you will keep it, my lord."

Jaq drew in a sharp breath.

Beresford's lips pressed together, for once showing a marked degree of unease. "Pardon me, Your Majesty?"

"The fact that you have the Star indicates Jaq trusts you. I find I do too, given your thick-headed loyalty and sense of honour towards both my undeserving children. Also, I know a little bit about your activities and your noble service to your own Crown. You will be interested to know that the selkie people are also opposed to the French navy's recent activities and excessive proliferation. I am hoping we can work towards a possible alliance with the English Crown."

Beresford blinked. "Oh? I am glad to hear it, Your Majesty, and I am certain my king will be amenable. However, it is not necessary to sacrifice your son's autonomy in pursuit of it."

"You misunderstand me," she replied. "It would not be a sacrifice."

Jaq frowned. So much for being his mother's favourite.

Beresford searched for words. "That may be so, Your Majesty, however …"

She interrupted, tilting her head graciously. "My lord, I believe my son might be a useful addition to your crew. Even now, Frenchmen are converging on your ship's hiding place, and you will need our help to remove with all haste." Beresford stiffened, but she did not allow him to interrupt. "Jaq's ability to be a seal might prove advantageous in your little quests. However, it is true somebody needs to teach him how to cut line. I think it might be you." She paused. "Of course, you will be obliged to care for Jaq as well: feed and shelter him, but that need not be anything more than you would already accord a member of your crew."

"Your Majesty, with respect …"

The queen's voice hardened. "You may not like the arrangement, my lord, but you are in a difficult position. Humans who have seen and heard so much of the selkies and merpeople are not allowed to return to land. Or if they are, they must take the Lethe and forget all. Would you prefer that?"

Beresford looked as if he might very well prefer it. However, after a moment's contemplation, his innate respect for his own mind reasserted itself. "No, Your Majesty."

"I did not think so," said the queen gently. "Jaq might be useful, you know, once you take him in hand."

Jaq was listening indignantly, but a thought occurred to him. He had always wanted to go ashore. Never at the cost of his own autonomy, but perhaps it would be good to hie away from Skerry for a while, even under these terms. Especially after Seraphine's birthday, and now this: the selkies would be rife with gossip and ridicule directed towards their High Prince. Furthermore, if he refused this punishment, what else would his mother replace it with? The mind boggled.

"For how long?" Jaq demanded.

The queen smiled. "As long as it takes, my son. When you have learned some discipline and restraint, and you aren't so fond of coral cutthroat."

Jaq doubted he would ever lose his affection for coral cutthroat, but he bowed his head. With any luck, he would have a land holiday with the earl for a couple of weeks while the scandal blew over. Then he could come back to the sea when everything had settled down. "Very well, Mother. I will surrender myself to the guidance of his lordship."

Beresford, still shivering, did not look as if he believed this humble acquiescence for a moment but was too cold to argue. "Very well, Your Majesty. I will take custody of his highness. I must admit, I am in need of an extra crew member. But I must ask one thing."

"What is that?"

"Clothes for his majesty."

"Of course," said the queen graciously. "Devonshire is not prepared for a naked selkie."

Jaq thought this might be true. Especially not one as good-looking as him.

THE END

The fun continues ...

Thanks for reading *The Selkie Scandal*! If you enjoyed it, I'd really appreciate it if you left a review on your platform of choice. Reviews really help new books, and new authors, find their readers.

If you want to read more about Beresford and Jaq's adventures in Devon, the Lady Diviner series will soon be releasing on all platforms, starting with *The Lady Jewel Diviner* (Book 1), and continuing with *The Moria Pearls* (Book 2) and *The Sapphire Library* (Book 3).

Join my newsletter to be kept up to date! You will also receive a free copy of another prequel novella to the series: *A Pendant for Trouble*, which introduces Miss Elinor Avely and her secret ability to divine the presence of jewels. Sign up at rosalieoaks.com/newsletter.

And you can always find me on social media if you want to chat about jam, the Regency era, or books!

Happy reading,

Rosalie

Join my newsletter for another prequel, this time telling of Beresford's first attempt to win Miss Elinor Avely, at a ducal garden party near London. Though I should warn you, the course of true love does not always run smooth!

A mysterious pendant, a distracting earl, an unfolding scandal ...

Miss Elinor Avely can't resist the call of a large jewel mysteriously concealed at a ducal garden party. After all, if the Earl of Beresford isn't attending, what else is Elinor to do with herself? Her talent for divining jewels can be an intriguing distraction for once, instead of a carefully guarded family secret.

Of course, her hunt for the jewel leads her straight into a mystery – and worse, an undignified encounter with Beresford. Yet when Elinor's quest goes from unseemly to scandalous, he is the one who tries to save her.

The question is: will she let him?

A Pendant for Trouble is where the magic, mystery, and romance all begins ...

Sign up for your free and exclusive copy at rosalieoaks.com/newsletter

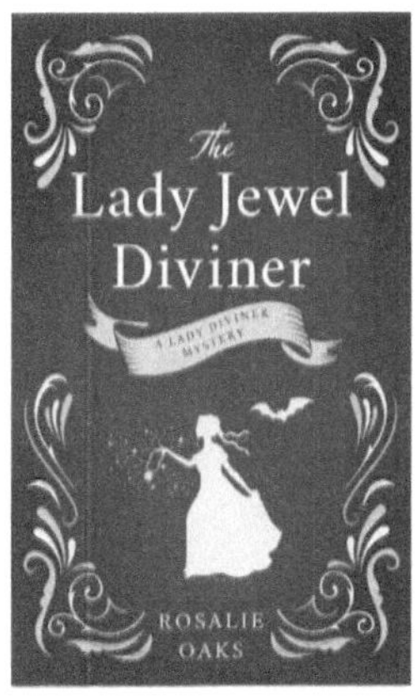

The Lady Jewel Diviner
Book 1 in the Lady Diviner series

Diamonds, Death, and Devonshire tea ... in a magical Regency England

Miss Elinor Avely's proper upbringing cannot prepare her for the tiny, spinster vampire who crashes into her sitting room and demands to be fed with a sheep.

Elinor already has enough troubles without having to catch ruminants. First, her secret gift for divining jewels has landed her in scandal, exiling her from London society. Second, a nobleman of dubious repute wants her to find a cache of smuggled jewels, hidden somewhere along the Devon coastline. Last – and worst – she is invited to cream tea at the local manor. And while the autocratic and magnificent Earl of Beresford might be there (and perhaps the jewels themselves too), Beresford is the last person Elinor wants to meet over cream tea.

When a dead body is discovered along the cliffs, of course, such delicate considerations become secondary. Fortunately, Elinor now has a small vampiric chaperone – even if said spinster has a habit of appearing stark naked – and together they are ready to risk the hard questions.

Where are the jewels hidden? Who killed the smuggler? And just when *is* the cream tea being served?

The Lady Jewel Diviner is the first book in a new historical mystery series, set in Regency England with generous servings of magic, manners, and romance.

Turn the page for an excerpt from Chapter One …

The Lady Jewel Diviner

Chapter One

In which a spinster vampire introduces herself to Elinor

Diamonds or cream tea? Miss Elinor Avely contemplated this difficult choice in the abstract as she stood in her new sitting room, holding two invitations in her hands. She concluded (rather quickly) that, in her case, fresh clotted cream would theoretically trump diamonds. Cream was *always* enjoyable, whereas diamonds were simply distracting for one such as she.

Cream tea, then.

Elinor pursed her lips. However, in this instance the invitation was issued by the Countess of Beresford, which made the matter more complicated.

Placing the thick paper on the dresser, Elinor eyed the red sealing wax. Tea with the Countess of Beresford would be … fraught. The countess was the earl's mother, after all, and it wasn't good etiquette to receive comestibles from a family when you had blackened their name with scandal.

Elinor sighed. That left her the diamond hunt.

The other letter, with its provocative proposition, was still in her other hand. She considered the foolscap with its scrawled handwriting, knowing what her answer *ought* to be. She certainly had not exiled herself, her brother, and her mother to the wilds of remote Devon so she could use her special gift to search for lost diamonds. That was the kind of thing that had landed Elinor in trouble in the first place.

So, no diamonds either. It was going to be a sorry existence, out here in Devon. Unless Napoleon invaded; that might make things more interesting.

She put the letter down next to the countess's invitation. Then she paused. Better to keep the letter about diamonds out of sight, especially from her mother, who was always so anxious to keep Elinor's gift a secret. Opening a Radcliffe novel, she slipped the letter between the pages – Mother wouldn't dare be seen opening *The Mysteries of Udolpho* – and closed the book with a snap.

Unfortunately, out of sight was not out of mind.

Elinor looked around the sitting room of their cottage, trying to be grateful for the refuge. It was on the edge of known civilisation, but at least their new residence was cosy and warm. She sank onto an armchair and looked out the window. Outside, the view was barren: the lonesome horizon of the Devon coastline, with hills hunched against ocean gales.

Out of habit, she was dressed for dinner in a high-waisted pale sage gown, one which she had purchased in London because it suited her honey-blonde hair and hazel eyes. Of course, they wouldn't receive any callers here at Casserly Cottage. In a way, Elinor was glad, for it gave her time to recover from the London debacle. Regrettably, it also gave her too much time to think about the earl.

The Earl of Beresford wasn't the handsomest man she'd ever met, she reflected, but he had the broadest shoulders and the most striking grey eyes. Was that the sum of his attraction? There was, of course, his nicely tapered waist to consider, his intelligent sense of humour, and his utter disregard for debutantes. All of which, somehow, made him irresistible. A pity she had managed to drag his name through the mud – though she was sure the Earl of Beresford would recover his reputation more quickly than she would.

Pressing her lips together, Elinor decided that a divination *would* be a good distraction. Would it do any harm to see, for curiosity's sake, if there were any diamonds hidden nearby? Mother need not know she had used her gift only briefly. Elinor's brother, Peregrine, was out walking, and the two servants – a housemaid and a cook – were busy cleaning up after dinner, while Mother read upstairs.

Elinor crossed to the window and peered outside. Between two hills was a stretch of rough sea on which a distant ship battled the waves. The sky, however, was glorious: piles and swirls of clouds, reflecting the last of the sun. Momentarily, she swept her inner sense over the scene below, as far as she could reach. No diamonds. With a shrug, she closed off that part of her mind and leaned desultorily against the edge of the window.

A shadow of a bat flitted across the garden. Elinor raised her hand to pull the curtains shut and saw a white, swooping barn owl hurtle out of the blackness. Catching her breath, she watched the owl's lethal power as it hunted the bat.

The white shape of the owl veered suddenly upwards. Then, as she watched, a small black shape shot out of the gloom and thudded into the window.

There was a horrible *thwack* and it dropped like a stone.

Elinor murmured in distress and bent to look at the creature that lay sprawled on the wooden sill. She blinked. It appeared to be pale white, not black as she had thought, and more like a tangle of limbs than a tangle of wings. She paused, and quickly snatched the iron key out of the dresser door. Her brother would laugh, but now Elinor was armed to her satisfaction. Slowly, she opened the window.

A tiny, white face lay against the wood, partially obscured by an upflung arm and a swirl of black hair. Elinor drew a breath. The creature was a girl, or woman, no larger than Elinor's hand. Furthermore, the woman was completely naked. Elinor shivered. The evening was cool, so she hastily pulled out a linen handkerchief to throw over the little person. As Elinor did so, the creature's eyes fluttered open.

"Arrggh. Cursed owls." She blinked at Elinor with deep blue eyes and tried to sit up. "Good evening."

"Good evening." Elinor was glad to hear her own voice was firm.

"I apologise for this irregular visit." The creature glanced down and pulled the linen closer around herself. "And for my lack of accoutrement."

Elinor gathered herself, though her heart was beating rapidly. At least this was a distraction from jewel divining. "Do you require some help?"

"I am a little indisposed," admitted the miniature lady. Her accent was odd, with a faint trace of French, but it spoke of noble breeding. "I will recover if I rest a while."

"Would you like to come inside? It will be warmer."

The lady spotted the iron key in Elinor's hand and her expression suddenly sharpened. "What is that? Do you mistake me for the fae?"

Embarrassed, Elinor hastily hid the key in the folds of her skirt.

"I tell you I am no such thing," snapped the lady.

"I apologise. I was not sure what kind of – er – personage was – er – calling upon me, and I thought it best to be cautious." Elinor paused, hoping the creature would enlighten her.

"Well, I am not fae. If you don't believe me, put that key against me. I won't shriek and die."

"I am sure that is not necessary," said Elinor, though she hesitated. Everyone knew the fae were notoriously given to trickery. That is, if they even existed.

The linen handkerchief rustled in indignation. "It is necessary, because you think I am trying to fool you."

Elinor narrowed her eyes. "If putting the key upon you will calm your nerves, I will do it." She held the iron up and moved it towards the little woman, who glared at her but showed no other signs of distress. Reluctantly, Elinor placed the key against her tiny hand.

The woman raised her brows and pursed her lips.

"Very well," said Elinor. "I am satisfied you are not fae. However, I might as well tell you – I don't believe in the fae."

"Oh, is that so? Lucky you. They are nasty creatures, rude and ill-bred."

"Will you tell me your name?"

"I am Miss Aldreda Zooth. I do apologise for the
lack of proper introduction. Normally I would obtain
one via my queen, but she is in France. I hope." A
frown crossed the pale face.

"I am Miss Elinor Avely."

They stared at each other in the twilight. Eventually Miss Zooth smiled. "You seem singularly calm for
someone who does not believe in the fae."

"You have just assured me that you are not fae."

"No, but I am a vampiri."

"I am afraid I do not know what that is."

Miss Zooth looked cross again. "Hmph. We are
magical and useful. And polite, even if my current
state of dress indicates otherwise."

Elinor cleared her throat. "Please do come in, Miss
Zooth. May I assist you?"

The miniature lady tried to stand, clutching the
handkerchief around her, but her legs were too weak.
She collapsed in a heap again. "Perhaps if you carry
me? I promise not to bite."

The little face turned away, eyes closed. Elinor felt
a stab of pity. "Shall I gather you up?"

Miss Zooth nodded, and Elinor carefully scooped
her up. She was light as a bird and seemed oddly frail.
Elinor bore her into the house and placed her on a

settee, pulling the primrose coloured shawl from her shoulders to tuck around her visitor. Miss Zooth tried to sit but struggled to hold herself up.

"Can I fetch you some tea? Some food?"

"Please."

Elinor strode quickly to the kitchen, where she fetched the teapot and cups herself rather than disturb the servants – who would be doubly disturbed if they saw the impossible Miss Zooth. She snatched up a bread roll and a chunk of cheese. What cup would serve? After a moment's thought she detoured to her sewing basket to obtain a thimble.

Miss Zooth accepted it gratefully, though it was more like a large mug in her hands. She took dainty sips and eyed the bread and cheese.

"I don't suppose you have any meat?" she asked. "I know it is rude to request it, but when I am this weak it is the best thing for me."

"I can find some corned beef. I believe we have some in the kitchen." Elinor stood again.

Miss Zooth shook her head, looking embarrassed. "Do you have any ... raw meat?"

"I am not sure," said Elinor. She looked at her curiously. "I don't know what the cook has in store. Her shopping day is tomorrow, so I fear we may be out of fresh meat."

Her visitor's shoulders sank a little. "I may have to leave soon, to find some."

"You are not fit to go anywhere." Elinor paused. "I am curious as to what sort of creature requires raw meat."

Miss Zooth lifted her head and looked Elinor squarely in the eye. "I require the blood of others to live. It is an unfortunate aspect of my nature."

Elinor considered this. "You practice … dark arts?"

"No doubt you eat meat," said the vampiri sharply. "It is not so different. I merely need it fresh. With – er – blood."

"What kind of blood?" Elinor had an uneasy feeling that humans were not excluded. She had vague recollections of such beings from old stories. In fact, she had recently seen a stone depiction of something similar: a small woman with bat wings.

Miss Zooth currently had no wings, however, and Elinor had not imagined that a dark creature would have deep blue eyes, a pert nose, and finely shaped hands. The vampiri's black hair curled softly over her shoulders, and her skin was a delicate white, almost translucent. She seemed rather more vulnerable than terrifying.

"I can make do with sheep," said Miss Zooth. "There are plenty of those around here. Or cows, if I have to. I don't like to take from small creatures, as it leaves them weak." She brightened. "I don't suppose you have a large dog, do you?"

Elinor blinked. "No, I'm afraid I cannot offer you a dog."

Miss Zooth looked disappointed.

"What about a cat?" suggested Elinor. "There is a cat who lives here." The large cream-coloured tom – named Samuel – lazed around the garden during the day and conducted mysterious business at night. He and Elinor were becoming friends, so she hesitated to offer him as Miss Zooth's snack. But the health of a small lady surely warranted more than a cat's dignity.

"I am afraid I would leave a cat somewhat incommoded," said Miss Zooth. "Besides, cats generally don't like me, and they are hard to catch." She swallowed and sank back into the shawl. "I fear I am at rather a low ebb. I must leave soon and find something."

Elinor regarded her thoughtfully. Then the front door opened, and Peregrine's voice floated through the house.

"Elinor? You'll never guess what I just saw."

She moved quickly to the sitting room door, blocking the entrance. "What, brother?"

The Lady Jewel Diviner releases on all platforms soon.
Join Rosalie's newsletter to be the first to hear about it,
at rosalieoaks.com/newsletter.

Rosalie Oaks writes novels set in a paranormal Regency England, with side servings of jam, jewels, and the occasional outrageous breach of propriety. As a child, she loved conducting home-made theatre productions with her three younger brothers. Now she directs her characters instead, but like her brothers, they don't always do what she says.

Rosalie wants to live in a world where scones are good for you, cream is slimming, and she can make the perfect jam. While writing, however, she contents herself with vast quantities of tea and chocolate.

The Lady Diviner series

A Pendant for Trouble (a prequel novella)

The Lady Jewel Diviner (Book 1)

The Moria Pearls (Book 2)

The Sapphire Library (Book 3)